Murder Miscalculated

by

Andrew MacRae

Mainly Murder Press, LLC

PO Box 290586
Wethersfield, CT 06129-0586
www.mainlymurderpress.com

Mainly Murder Press

Copy Editor: Jack Ryan
Executive Editor: Judith K. Ivie
Cover Designer: Karen A. Phillips

Copyright © 2014 by Andrew MacRae
Paperback ISBN 978-0-9913628-2-0
E-book ISBN 978-0-9913628-3-7

Published in the United States of America

Mainly Murder Press
PO Box 290586
Wethersfield, CT 06129-0586
www.MainlyMurderPress.com

Dedication

For the real Barbara and Doris,
family and friends, and Susannah

Also by Andrew MacRae:

Murder Misdirected

One

My wallet was gone.

It had been stolen out of my jacket without my noticing a thing. I controlled a frantic impulse to check the other pockets of my suit, along with an equally strong wish to kick myself. I kept my hands where they were and concentrated on figuring out when and where it could have happened.

I was standing in front of a book dealer's table on the grassy field at Fort Williams. The annual used book show was in full swing, and a sea of dealers' booths surrounded me. Bright nylon sunshades on poles protected the books and the vendors from the glare of the afternoon sun and covered the grassy grounds with color. Under each tent were rows of tables stacked with used books, rare books and worthless books. Pickings were slim, as it was the last afternoon of the show. I'm a conservative buyer, so I had only half a dozen books in the knapsack on my shoulder. The sun warmed my shoulders, and the sounds and smells of the bay filled the air.

Fort Williams is an old, decommissioned US Army embarkation facility on the bay that had been transformed into a popular outdoor park and center of events. The voices of two million men who had sailed off into the Pacific War so many decades ago were now replaced by the cries of swirling seagulls competing with fanciful kites for airspace overhead. A strong breeze rippled the sunshades and carried the tolling of bells on buoys anchored in the bay. Those maritime sounds blended with calls and shouts from a nearby soccer match, children on a nearby playground, the sound of city traffic and the chatter of several thousand avid book lovers. The breeze also brought a heady fragrance of fish and saltwater mixed with the scent of new-mown grass from the playing fields.

When could my wallet have been taken?

In my head I retraced my route among the crowded tables. I had just come from Sartain's Rare Books, and before that Dupin's. That was it, Dupin's New & Used Books. I had been looking at a first edition Perry Mason from 1954 when someone brushed up against me. I hadn't given it any thought at the time, but that had to be when my wallet disappeared. I tried to conjure up an image of the person who had done it, but all I remembered was an arm reaching past me, an arm clothed in brown tweed with a leather patch on the elbow. I shook my head as a wave of chagrin washed over me. A year ago, before I gave up picking pockets, it never would have happened.

I put the book I was looking at, a Craig Rice novel from the early forties with the dust jacket in fair condition, back on the table and slowly turned around. I scanned the people around me, trying not to let my concern show in my face. There was no one with a tweed jacket in sight.

I asked the dealer if I could park my knapsack with him for a few minutes. Paul knew me and agreed.

"You want me to put this away for you?" He held up the Craig Rice.

"Go ahead and leave it out. I'll be back in a few minutes." I wanted the book, but if I couldn't get my wallet back, I would have to head home with my pride well and duly dinged.

I put myself in the pickpocket's position, not exactly a difficult thing for me to do, given my former profession. If I had lifted a wallet over by Dupin's table, I would have headed toward the refreshment stands. Far more people were over there, and it was at the edge of the event in case a quick getaway was needed. Also, if I were the pickpocket, I would be looking for someone looking for me, so following straight in his footsteps was not going to work.

Instead I went at a right angle to my destination, walking slowly and stopping for a moment at each table, exchanging greetings if I knew the dealer and scanning through the titles on display as though nothing was amiss. I reached a dealer who had banners on one side of his booth, protecting his vintage and fragile sheet music from the breeze. I shrugged off my coat as I passed behind the banners and draped it over my arm. I emerged from their shadow and continued to the next booth, one that specialized in science fiction.

I found a copy of *Starlog Magazine* from the mid-1970s with a photo of a grinning George Pal sitting in The Time Machine on the cover. I bought it with the few loose dollars I had left in my pocket and bent my face down close to the magazine as I walked away as if giving it intense study. I let my shoulders drop and my knees give a little at the same time. I had now changed my outward appearance, height and manner of walking. Those are the visual cues we all use when watching for someone, and if I was lucky, it would be enough to fool my pickpocket.

I reached the end of the row of dealer booths and headed toward the refreshment stands, still scanning the crowd from behind the magazine.

A book fair attracts all sorts of people. I saw a Mulligan stew of the American public, milling about while looking at books, talking about books, buying books and selling books. I continued my search.

I passed a bearded, leather-clad Goth haggling over an early edition of *The Bell Jar* with a geriatric beatnik woman. He must have outweighed the woman by a good two hundred pounds, but she was his match in spirit as they competed over who would get the best bargain.

At another booth a buttoned-down corporate dude perused a collection of Manga comics, shoulder to shoulder with long-haired teens in ragged jeans and torn tee shirts. Still farther along, a man with a toddler in a backpack and an infant in a front sling sorted through a large collection of *National Geographic Magazines.*

I saw people of every age, wearing clothes of most every style and color, but no one I saw wore a brown tweed jacket with leather patches on the elbows. I wondered if I had lost my wallet for good and began to take inventory in my head of what was in it and what would need stopping or replacing. Still I kept walking, searching and scanning the crowd.

Finally I hit pay dirt.

He stood about thirty feet in front of me near a seated trio of two violinists and a cellist playing a jazzed-up version of a classical piece. The guy was young, perhaps in his mid-twenties with short blond hair, a wide, full face, about my height but with more muscle. He was dressed in a preppy style that I never cared for – a tweed jacket over a dress shirt, khaki slacks and canvas deck shoes. He stood in profile to me, looking back in the direction of Dupin's tables, possibly checking to see if I had twigged to my wallet being gone. In one hand he carried a shopping bag, and I was confident with the certainty of experience that my wallet would be somewhere within it. I kept walking toward him, continuing to use the magazine to hide my face.

I was within two steps of my quarry before he realized it, and even then he showed no signs of recognizing me as he tried to step out of my way. We collided, and I hooked his left leg to make certain he came down with my contrived fall. In two seconds we were on the ground in a Gordian knot of arms and legs. The musicians stopped playing, and people turned to watch us.

"Hey!"

"I'm sorry," I mumbled while clumsily grasping and letting go of his wrist, his arms and the lapels of his coat as I tried to regain my footing. We got to our feet at the same time. I bent over to pick up my magazine. I let him get a good look at my face as I straightened. He gave a start of recognition and began to say something, but he seemed to realize people were watching us. The last thing a pickpocket needs is a crowd of people looking at him.

"Sorry," I said again as the musicians resumed playing, and people lost interest in the scene. I walked away, letting my body straighten out to its normal height. On reaching a table near the refreshment stand, I put down the magazine and slipped my jacket back on. Then I looked back at him. As I expected, he was watching me.

It was time to let my young friend know what was what.

I held a wallet up for him to see. I smiled as he patted each of his pockets as if unwilling to believe what he saw. I dropped his wallet onto the table and nonchalantly took a seat with my back to him.

It took him two minutes to make up his mind. I timed him. I looked up as he came around the table and faced me. His eyes darted from side to side as he tried to figure out how to play the scene, then he reached for his wallet. I put my hand on top of it before he could snag it and shook my head.

"Nope. Even trade or nothing."

His shoulders drooped. "Okay." He sat down in a chair opposite me and began fishing in the paper bag. He brought out several wallets, one at a time and holding them low, near the top of the bag, until I spotted mine. I nodded, and he set it on the table.

I let go of his wallet and picked up mine. He grabbed his wallet, and we both checked the contents before stowing them back in our respective pockets.

I found him studying my face.

"Hey, I know you," he said. "I've seen you before. You're The Kid, aren't you?"

"Close. I used to be The Kid. I'm out of the business these days."

"I'm Chad," he offered, not that I was interested. "How come you quit? Everyone says you were the best."

Gah. It wouldn't have been easy to explain to him, nor did I have an inclination to do so. As far as I was concerned, The Kid was dead and buried. "Let's just say I found a better gig," I said.

I saw how well dressed he was and put two and two together. "You're one of Doris Whitaker's crew, aren't you?"

He was offended. "I work for Mrs. Whitaker." He emphasized his employer's title.

I waved a hand. "Sorry. It's just that I've heard so many stories about when Doris, I mean Mrs. Whitaker, was only a hugger mugger."

I couldn't tell from the expression on Chad's face if he was more offended at my being on first name terms with his boss or my claim that she used to roll drunks, not that it mattered to me. I didn't bother to tell him that Doris had tried to recruit me back when I was his age. I got up and made to leave.

Chad leaned back and gave a laugh. "Just think, I boosted The Kid's wallet. Guess it's a good thing you quit when you did."

"Yeah," I said. "Good thing. With competition like you I wouldn't stand a chance." He smiled with smug satisfaction.

I took a step away and then turned back. I really didn't like the smirk on his face. "Hey, Chad, you wouldn't happen to know what time it is, would you?"

He stuck out his left arm and let the cuff ride up. His wrist was bare. He looked at me, his eyes wide. I tossed his watch down on the table and left.

God, that felt good.

Two

"You got your wallet stolen? Gee, what a shame." I could see Lynn was trying not to smile. Barbara was nice enough to take a sudden interest in the ceiling.

I glared at Lynn. "It's not funny."

Lynn, Barbara and I sat at the table in the back room-kitchen of our store, The Book Nook. It's a bookstore often described by our customers as eclectic and almost as often described as eccentric. We are open twenty-fours a day, unless we feel like closing up for a few hours. The store is on the ground floor of an old three-story brownstone on Knickerbocker Lane, a mostly forgotten side street in the heart of downtown.

"Well," chimed in Barbara with more than a trace of a smile on her ancient, wise face. "You have to admit there's a certain poetic justice in it, Greg."

I tried to glare at Barbara, but that's not really possible. Barbara Jenkins is my oldest friend, both in the number of years I have known her and in age. Lynn and I bought the store and the building from Barbara when we got married a year ago. I manage the bookstore while Lynn gives lessons in a dance studio on the third floor. A condition of our purchase was that Barbara stayed on living there with us. Neither Lynn nor I nor any of our customers could imagine The Book Nook without Barbara's comforting presence.

It was close to eight in the evening, and we were eating our supper. We usually ate around then. Lynn, Barbara and I are night owls by nature, and these unhurried, late night meals give us a chance to compare and catch up our calendars, and unwind.

It was Barbara's turn to prepare supper that day, and the kitchen was filled with the smell of homemade soup and bread.

We had already finished off a colorful garden salad that Barbara called a wildflower salad. It was made with arugula, nasturtium blossoms and kale, topped with shredded Brussels sprouts and Barbara's homemade poppy seed dressing.

I buttered another piece of wheat bread, baked by Barbara that afternoon, and explained to my two best friends what had happened that afternoon at the used book show.

I noticed that Lynn was watching my hand as I finished the story. I looked down and only then realized I was flipping a teaspoon between my fingers, an exercise I learned to do in the old days to keep my fingers nimble. Strangely, I couldn't remember the last time I had done that.

Lynn raised her eyes to mine and I could read concern in them.

"Hey," I said. I put the spoon down, reached over and took her hand in mine. "Don't worry, I'm not going back into the pickpocket business."

She squeezed my fingers. "I hope not, Greg."

An awkward silence followed as the three of us relived memories from the previous year, memories each would rather not resurrect. Barbara, Lynn and I had almost lost our lives because of my picking pockets, and it would be an understatement to say that the experience had scared me straight.

We were saved from our thoughts by the ringing of the bell over the shop's front door and a familiar voice calling out a greeting. A minute later Old Tom pushed through the beaded curtain that separated the bookstore from the back room. Junior, the bookstore cat, lay across Tom's shoulders. "Good evening, everyone. Is that soup I smell?"

Tom was our volunteer store clerk from nine in the evening until daybreak. He tended the store counter through the night in exchange for supper, all the books he could read, and a refuge from the world. Tom was a part-time deacon at Saint Timothy's, an Episcopal church a few blocks away. He wore his gray hair long, and his bald spot was forever covered by a cloth slouch cap. He peered at the world through impossibly small wire frame glasses with a slight blue tint in the lenses. Tom was typical of the community of customers our store attracted.

Barbara hopped up, took Junior from Tom's shoulders and placed him on the floor. Junior, a large Russian Blue who believed he was the real owner of the store, ignored the rest of us and strolled in his easy way over to his food dish. Barbara gave Tom a hug and set a place for him at the table. "You bet it's soup," she said as she ladled some into the bowl she placed in front of him. "Have a taste, and see if you can figure out what I put in it."

Tom lifted a spoonful to his mouth and slowly savored it. "Beef, of course, wild rice, some ginger and," he paused, "fennel, right?"

"Right!" Barbara was pleased. She patted her braids, neatly coiled around her head. With her sundress and sandals Barbara's look harkened back to an age of flower-power, peace marches and protest.

When we finished eating Tom went up front to watch the store while Barbara, Lynn and I turned to our nighttime chores. It was my job that evening to wash the dishes with Lynn drying. I tried to keep up a light banter, but Lynn did not respond to my gibes. Her long, dark hair hid her face from me, but her silence and body language told me that my run-in with Chad, the young pickpocket, had unsettled her.

The dishes done, I spent the next hour at the desk by the wall, with Junior on my lap, his deep purr more felt than heard. I had learned over the previous year that running a bookstore takes a frightful amount of paperwork. Lynn sat at the table and worked out the schedule for an upcoming series of dance classes. Barbara and Tom were in the store, chatting with a customer.

This was my favorite time of the day. The three of us had formed a comfortable routine. We weren't rolling in dough, as the bookstore business and making money seem to be forever at odds, but at least we were covering our expenses and doing what we wanted.

Lynn's dance studio on the third floor of the old brownstone provided the extra income that made things possible. During the morning she offered classes for soccer moms and seniors. Afternoons were filled with children of all ages, and twice a week she offered evening classes for exotic dancers, strippers and more than a few housewives looking to spice up their marriages.

Barbara used the studio, too, for her twice-a-week early morning yoga and meditation classes, having given up teaching tap dancing a few years before when she graduated from septuagenarian to octogenarian.

As for me, I kept us stocked in new and used books and handled the online orders that were coming with increasing frequency. Tonight there was a stack of books to put in packages and, in the morning, taken to the post office.

Lynn and I finished our paperwork chores about the same time. I poured two glasses of cold white wine, and we took them out into the store. We made ourselves comfortable in the twin easy chairs we provide for our customers. Junior saw us and jumped down from a nearby bookshelf. He walked over, climbed into my lap and began washing himself.

Lynn read a dance magazine, occasionally turning back the corner of a page to mark an article to save. I paged through the latest issue of *Publishers Weekly*, mentally making notes of new books.

At eleven Barbara came out to say goodnight to everyone. Lynn and I finished our wine and said goodnight to Tom. Junior's tail twitched in protest when I placed him on the hardwood floor. Then he silently slipped away to begin his nighttime prowl.

Late that night, after Lynn and I had retired to our room on the second floor, I lay awake in the darkness as lights and shadows crept across the walls and ceiling. Outside the mullioned, iron-framed windows, the streets of the city carried on with their late-night ways. I suspected from the sound of her breathing that Lynn was awake, too. She must have sensed I wasn't asleep.

"Greg? Are you awake?"

I rolled over toward her. "Yes. You, too?"

"Yes." She lifted a hand, reached over and touched the tips of her fingers to my cheek. "I'm worried about you. I'm worried that you miss working the street."

I forced a laugh. "Don't worry. There's no way I'm going back to that kind of life." I took her hand from my face and kissed her fingers. "Why should I? I have everything I want right here."

She took her hand away from mine and raised herself up on her elbow. In the fragmented light I could see a shadow, not cast by any physical object, cross her face. "Greg, I'm serious. I'm worried you might be tempted too much by," she paused, searching for words, "by your old way of life, by your life as The Kid. And you need to know something." Her voice had a quiet urgency. "If you do go back, I don't know that we can stay together."

I felt as if the shadow that had crossed Lynn's face had passed through me. If there was one thing I had learned from the events of the previous year, it was that Lynn meant more to me than anything.

I lifted myself up onto my elbow, matching Lynn's pose. I reached over and stroked her hair, then her face. "Lynn, I promise. I'm done with picking pockets. I'm done with all of that. I promise."

Lynn started to say something, then nestled back down onto her pillow. "I hope so. For everyone's sake, I hope so."

I lay back down next to her, my arm around her. In a few minutes she was asleep.

I stayed awake long into the night, listening to the sounds of the street outside and unable to will myself to sleep. I truly meant what I'd told Lynn. I really was through with my old life as a pickpocket.

Or so I thought.

Three

Trouble walked into The Book Nook at a quarter past ten the next morning.

I was on the rolling bookshelf ladder, standing with my head up near the whitewashed, stamped tin ceiling, dusting the books on the upper shelves. Junior sunned himself on a ledge under a store window as he supervised my work. A selection of '40s swing tunes played on the stereo, and I was moving in time with the music while trying not to sneeze as dust motes swirled around my head.

The shop door opened and the bell over it jingled.

"I'll be with you in a minute," I called over Artie Shaw's keening clarinet without looking behind me.

"Take your time. I can wait." There was an edge in the man's voice that caused me to leave the dusting until later and attend to him.

I gave him the eye as I came down the ladder, well aware that he was watching me in return. He looked to be on the far side of forty. He was heavyset without being overweight and wore a conservative dark suit. His well-groomed dark hair had a touch of gray, and his face was clean-shaven. There was an intensity in his eyes that reminded me of the way a dog studies someone new. Perhaps Junior felt the same way, as he came from his place in the storefront window and joined me behind the counter.

My visitor quickly dispelled any notion that he was a customer by displaying an FBI badge and identity card as he stated more than asked, "Mr. Gregory Smith, I presume."

I switched off the stereo. "Yes, that's me. What can I do for you?"

The man took a moment to slip his identification holder back inside his jacket pocket before answering. His right pocket, I couldn't help noticing. Old habits die hard.

"I'm Special Agent Lawrence Talbot. I've been told you have certain skills that may be of use to me."

I tried to keep my voice neutral. "How do you mean?"

"I need someone to teach a member of my team how to pick a pocket."

I shook my head. "I'm sorry, Agent Talbot, but it's no use. I'm done with that kind of work." I waved my arm. "See? I've got a bookstore to run."

"We could make it worth your while, or …" his voice trailed off.

I didn't like the sound of that. "Or what?"

"One year ago you were given a clean record, courtesy of my agency. That clean record could just as easily be rescinded." My stomach clenched. I don't like threats, veiled or otherwise. I had to choke back a reply before I said something I would likely regret. As I sought more temperate words, a voice came from the doorway to the back room.

"I don't think you heard what my husband said, Mr. Talbot."

Lynn pushed through the beaded curtain from the back room. She wore a black leotard, and her long, dark hair was down. As usual, she wore ballet slippers, and they made no sound as she stalked across the room. If Talbot reminded me of a dog, Lynn was a she-panther. I recognized the look on her face and would not want to be in Agent Talbot's position.

Lynn made no secret of the fact that she had been listening. She came behind the counter, took my arm and faced our unwelcome visitor. Her voice was cold. "Greg is through with that kind of work, and he's not going back to it, no matter what threats you make."

"Ah, Mrs. Smith, how nice to meet you in person. I enjoyed reading your file. I understand you no longer perform at The

Pink Poodle." Talbot let his eyes wander up and down Lynn's figure.

I started to move, and Lynn tightened her grip on my arm.

Talbot continued. "That's a shame. I wish I could have seen you. But you have kept your professional name, haven't you?" He pointed toward the sign that told visitors that the Lynn Vargas Dance Studio was two flights up. "Perhaps you are thinking of returning to stripping?"

I decided I really didn't like Special Agent Lawrence Talbot. "I believe you have our answer, Agent Talbot," I said, making my words final. "Thanks, but no thanks."

Talbot lifted his hands in a *well, I tried* gesture and turned to leave. When he reached the front door he stopped and looked back at us.

"It's too bad. Agent Cochran thought for certain you'd be willing to help him."

Damn and double damn. Of all the names he had to throw at us, it would be that one. Cochran had been in the thick of things last year and had proven himself to be a good and true friend. If he needed help, I would at least have to listen to what Talbot wanted of me. Lynn dug her fingers into my arm. I knew she shared my feeling about Cochran.

"Wait," I called. "You didn't tell me Cochran was involved."

Talbot's mouth tightened into a thin, humorless smile. "I thought dropping his name might help."

I ignored him and instead turned to Lynn. She searched my eyes as though looking for our future, and she looked troubled about what she saw. Then she dropped her eyes and nodded. I turned to Talbot.

"Okay. We'll listen to what you have to say, but we make no promises. Let's go into the back room, and you can tell us about it."

Talbot's smile broadened enough to show his teeth. "Trust me when I say that I ask for nothing more."

Lynn led the way through the beaded curtain. Talbot followed her, and I followed him. If a customer showed up, we'd hear the bell over the door. We sat at the table with Lynn and I sitting next to each other and Talbot across from us.

Our unwelcome visitor sniffed the air. There was fresh-brewed coffee on the stove, so Lynn must have been preparing it when Talbot arrived. Neither Lynn nor I offered him any. Our friends are welcome to share coffee with us anytime, but those who begin their acquaintance with threats go without. He must have sensed that as he turned his attention to us.

"Right," began Talbot, placing both hands on the table. "Here's the situation. My team is on the verge of busting a major fugitive, but to nail him we need to intercept some information. That information will be stored on a data card in a certain person's wallet. We want you to teach our agent enough pickpocketing skills that he can take the wallet without being detected."

I frowned. "Can't you just get a warrant for it?"

Talbot tugged his earlobe as he thought before answering. I wondered what sort of tell that was. Was he coming up with a plausible lie, or was he trying to decide how much he wanted us to know? After a few seconds he brought his hand back down to the table. "We need it to look like a random theft by someone working the street. We can't let the target have any reason to suspect that whoever took his wallet was after the data card."

"How will you know the right day to take the card?" asked Lynn.

Talbot shook his head. "I'm sorry, Ms. Vargas, but that information cannot be divulged. Suffice it to say that we will know with certainty."

"How much time do you have until this has to happen?" I asked, my mind working on the problem.

"One month."

I stared at the ceiling and mulled it over. One month to train someone to lift a wallet. If he or she wasn't too clumsy, it could be done.

"Where does Cochran fit into this?" Lynn asked.

"Agent Cochran is the one you'll be teaching."

I looked over at Lynn. She looked at Talbot.

"You said you could make it worth Greg's time."

"We can pay a consulting fee to compensate for the time he has to spend away from the bookstore." He named a figure that couldn't help but appeal to us.

"You said away from the store," said Lynn, ever the practical one. "Couldn't he teach Cochran here at The Book Nook?"

Talbot shook his head. "No, Agent Cochran is already undercover and has established a routine. You'll meet with him at Wykowski's Gym."

I knew that gym. It was down by what remained of the city's docks. I wondered what kind of undercover identity the normally button-down Cochran had assumed.

Talbot continued, "Cochran has established a routine of going there every morning for a couple of hours. We can arrange for a private room where you can work with him without anyone knowing what's going on."

"Why is Cochran working for you?" I asked. "Where's Agent Riley?" Riley was head of the team of agents I'd first tangled with, and then eventually worked with, in my previous occupation. Riley was also the one who had made it possible for me to start with a clean slate.

"Special Agent Riley is teaching a course back in Quantico, Virginia, for a few months. I've been assigned to lead his team in the meantime."

No one spoke. I studied Lynn's face, knowing how much she hated the idea of my getting mixed up in something like this. We had spent the past year working hard to build our new life. While neither of us wanted to see that work endangered, I couldn't help but feel that I should help Cochran if I could.

"It would be fun to see Cochran again," I offered.

Lynn ignored my comment and got up from the table, an angry look on her face. She shook her head. "If you want to do it, go ahead, just as long as you don't get involved in anything dangerous. The money's not worth it." She leaned over the table and tapped a long finger in front of our visitor.

"Agent Talbot."

"Yes, Ms. Vargas?"

"I want a letter on Bureau letterhead, signed by you, stating that the work for which you are hiring Greg is legal. No letter, no deal."

"You'll have it."

Lynn nodded and went up the stairs to her studio without saying another word. Part of me wanted to go after her and tell her the deal was off, but instead I listened to her footsteps on the stairs and the door slamming as she went into her dance studio.

It took only a few minutes for Talbot and me to work out the details. I'd meet Cochran at nine in the morning each weekday for the next month and spend an hour working with him. Talbot would arrange for a gym membership in my name. At my insistence he agreed to make it good for a full year and include a separate membership for Lynn. She and I had been talking about joining a gym anyway, and Wycowski's was a good one, if a bit far from The Book Nook.

Our business concluded, I walked with Talbot to the front door.

"Trust me, Mr. Smith," he said as he left. "You're making the right decision."

I thought about his words as the jingle from the bell above the door faded away and the store became quiet again.

Junior came back out from behind the counter, and I picked him up and held him in my arms. The late, great Fast Eddie Dupre once told me, "Kid, if someone tells you to trust them more than once in the same conversation, that's when you shouldn't."

"Did you hear him, Junior?" I asked the cat as I rubbed him between his ears. "He said we should trust him. I think I should trust him about as much as a mouse should trust you."

Junior didn't answer. He didn't have to.

Four

Later that day I headed up the stairs to the second floor. When I arrived on the landing I could hear Lynn in her dance studio one flight above me, giving commands to her early afternoon class of exercising women. "Now rotate, one, two, three."

I reached out as I walked down the narrow hallway and let my fingers run along the old wallpaper, feeling the texture and the places where it was peeling. A lingering trace of oily smoke reminded me, as it always does, that Lynn and I still have much work to do repairing and restoring the old building.

I was looking for a room that would suit my purpose. The second floor was a small warren of rooms, some reachable via the hallway, some found only by wandering through interconnecting doors. Most of the rooms on the second floor saw little use, and our very slow renovation of the building had yet to reach this floor except for two rooms at the front that Lynn and I had remodeled into a small bedroom suite. Barbara's own bedroom was downstairs off the kitchen, harkening back to when she'd lived here alone.

Halfway down the hall I pushed open a door whose hinges squeaked their need for oil. I fumbled on the wall for the light switch. It clicked loudly, and a single bare bulb in the ceiling lit up and illuminated a small, windowless room. Faded posters covered what wallpaper remained. The air smelled of dust, old clothes and time.

In the center of the room was what I was looking for, an old dressmaker's dummy that kept a lonely vigil over a clutter of dilapidated trunks and stacks of sagging cardboard boxes.

I draped the sports coat I was carrying around the dummy's shoulders, then stood back and contemplated it. It stood much too low to the floor for my purpose. I dragged a trunk over, picked up the dummy and placed it on top. My hands were covered in dust from the trunk and the dummy, and I wiped them off on an old shirt lying on top of one of the boxes. As I put the shirt back down I wondered whose it was and when it had last been worn.

I looked at the dummy again. Now it was a little too high, but it was good enough for what I needed.

I shook my head. If only Fast Eddie Dupre could see me having to go back to the basics. My guess is he'd be cackling that loopy laugh of his.

"No, not like that. Smooth, smooth like the way a copperhead glides through the swamp." Eddie took my wrist and pulled it back from the dummy wearing the coat. We were in the basement of his cheap apartment building. I was fifteen, a street kid who thought he was a pickpocket. Eddie had offered to take me under his wing and teach me the ancient art of picking pockets. "Now watch me," he commanded. I watched.

Eddie was in his early fifties back then, slicked-back black hair on the long side, handsome face showing his Cajun heritage and a body beginning to show the ravages of a life lived on the wrong side of the street. He took a few steps back and then walked across the basement as if going for a stroll on Bourbon Street in his native New Orleans. He glanced up at the dingy, pipe-lined ceiling as though admiring a cloudless, sunny sky. He looked to one side and waved and smiled at someone, perhaps a lady friend from his long-ago youth. He whistled a little, and then, when he was a few steps past the dummy, he stopped and turned and held up a wallet for me to see. It was the wallet I'd placed in the pocket of the jacket just a minute before.

"I never saw you take it," I said, amazed. "I was watching you the whole time, and I never saw you take it."

"You are wrong, my young friend. You thought you were watching me the whole time but I can guarantee you weren't. Otherwise you'd have seen me do the dip." He smiled at the confusion on my face. "Think back carefully, and then do what I did exactly, step by step."

I went over to the dark stone wall where Eddie had started and waited while he replaced the wallet in the jacket on the dummy. I took a step and stopped. "You want me to imitate the way you walked? I don't think I can."

"Sure you can, Kid. Think about how I held myself and how I moved."

I closed my eyes for a moment, visualizing Eddie's walk. Then I opened my eyes and began walking, swinging my arms a bit, sauntering as best I could the way Eddie had sauntered down his imaginary street.

"Stop," Eddie commanded. I froze in place. "You've got the walk and you've got the arms, but what about my head. What was my head doing while I walked?"

"You were looking from side to side," I answered.

"Then go back and start again and do the same."

I went back and started again, wondering if I was crazy for thinking this old guy could teach me to be a master pickpocket.

I gave it another try. I walked like Eddie had walked. I swung my arms like Eddie had swung his arms. I looked from side to side in that easy nonchalant way he had.

That was it. As I passed the dummy on my left I looked sharply to my right as though I had heard or seen something. At the same time, I let my left hand drop down and slip the wallet from the jacket without altering my arm's swinging motion. I kept walking and didn't break my stride until I reached the other side of the basement, then turned and held the wallet up for Eddie to see. He laughed when he saw the wide smile of triumph on my face.

"Very good, Kid, very good. You see, it's all a matter of misdirection. When you look to your right quickly like that, anyone watching you, anyone even slightly aware of you, is going to look over there, too. They can't help it."

That was the start of my training. I spent countless hours in that basement, walking past the dummy and taking its wallet over and over again. I learned to take a wallet from outside pockets and inside pockets. I learned how to scissor my fingers when plucking a wallet so that there was no visible movement in the tendons of my wrist. I graduated from working with the dummy to using Eddie as my victim. He'd put his wallet in one pocket or another without my watching and I had to find a way to steal it without his noticing, lest his hand come down on my wrist like iron.

"Hurts, doesn't it?" he'd say as he tightened his fingers. "That's what a pair of steel handcuffs are going to feel like if you get caught." He let go, and I massaged my wrist. "Remember that, Kid. If you get caught, it's all over."

His voice faded from my thoughts, and I found myself massaging my wrist as though Eddie had grabbed hold of it through almost twenty years of time.

"So this is where you took yourself, Greg."

Barbara's voice brought me back to the present. I turned and saw her standing in the doorway.

"Lynn told me about your visitor this morning and what he wants you to do." She peered at me with her wise eyes. "Are you sure this is the right thing to do?"

"Cochran needs my help, Barbara."

"I like Cochran as much as you do, Greg, but is helping him really the reason you are doing this? Or is it because you miss the excitement of being a pickpocket?"

I found myself unable to answer. Barbara walked over to me. She gently took both my hands and peered at my face with concern. She is at least a foot shorter than me, but to me it felt as if she was looking down at a child.

"Never mind," she said. "We all have to do what we're meant to do. Maybe this is what you are meant to do, or maybe it isn't. Only time will tell." Barbara reached up and gave me a kiss on the cheek. "I trust you to do the right thing."

She looked around the room, and my eyes followed hers. "Look at those posters, Greg. Relics of a time long ago, back when we wore flowers in our hair, bracelets, bells and bare feet, and we thought we could change the world."

The faded posters overlapped and covered the walls, leaving little of the original peeling wallpaper exposed. They dated from the late '60s through the mid-'70s and were filled with pop-art images, psychedelic flowers and young people wearing bellbottom pants, long hair and headbands. Several posters were stridently anti-war, anti-establishment and pretty much anti-everything else except free love.

"You know, Greg, back then my store served as a meeting place and a way station for the civil rights and anti-war movements." There was pride in Barbara's voice. "Oh, the times we had here. Everyone who was anyone in those days spent the night here at one time or another. On some nights every room in the building was filled with people. There was music everywhere, all kinds of food being cooked and planning for marches and protests at all hours of the day." Her smile broadened. "That's when The Book Nook began staying open all night." She swept her arm around. "If these rooms could talk, what stories they would tell."

She and I stood a minute in silence, listening to the past as it whispered to us, and then Barbara gave my hand a squeeze. "Well, I'd better let you get back to your practicing. You've probably got a lot to relearn." She turned and left the room, blowing me a kiss as she did. I listened to her soft steps on the old wood floor outside the room as she made her way back down the hallway.

I turned back to the dressmaker's dummy and adjusted the way the jacket hung on its shoulders. I ran my hands up and down the jacket while looking at the ceiling, at the posters on the wall, anywhere but at the jacket. I let my fingers explore each pocket surreptitiously, probing, removing the wallet from one pocket, placing it back in another and then repeating the process over and over, letting my muscle memory regain its surety.

Tomorrow morning I would take on the role Fast Eddie had taken with me and begin teaching Cochran the skills needed to pickpockets. I meant what I'd told his boss. I was confident that I could teach him to do what he needed in four weeks, three if he was a quick study. I was glad Barbara trusted me to do the right thing, and I hoped Lynn felt the same. I only wished I knew it, too.

Five

Early the next morning I walked a couple of blocks from Little Knickerbocker Lane into the morning rush hour bustling along Market Street. I joined the river of pedestrians and flowed with them until I came to where I was able to catch one of the vintage streetcars that ran on the F Line. It was painted a bold yellow and blue with a plaque that told me it had first hit the streets in the1940s. The interior was historically accurate to the era, as well, and smelled of leather and varnish. I rode standing up, holding tightly to the leather strap that hung from the overhead rail as we rolled and swayed across town and down toward the wharves. Above us the connectors on the roof snapped and clacked along the high-voltage overhead lines.

I got off the streetcar at Battery Street across and down the street from Wykowski's Gym. The buildings in that part of the city dated from the heyday of the sea trade. They were made of red brick and stone, three and four stories high, and sat right up against the sidewalks. Their mullioned, sash-and-counterweight windows had been replaced with energy efficient smoked glass panes that didn't open. The whole neighborhood, once the realm of stevedores and longshoremen, has become a high-tech ghetto, a place where caffeinated young workers slave over computer workstations and dream of winning the stock option lottery.

Except Wykowski's Gym.

Wykowski's Gym has squatted in the same location since the turn of the last century, and it's held fast to the old ways as if in defiance of the changes around it. The short, stout building boasts elaborate deco designs and is made of gleaming, white Portland cement. Along the side of the building I saw faded traces of painted advertisements still visible on its walls, promoting prizefights fought almost eighty years ago. I crossed the street and went inside.

A very fit man and a very fit woman, both wearing t-shirts so bright and unwrinkled that I half suspected they'd been ironed, were behind the desk in front of the main exercise room. They greeted me with bright smiles and found the passes arranged by Talbot for Lynn and me. They directed me to room 202, up the stairs and first door on the right, only after giving me an obligatory five-minute spiel about the joys of working out at Wykowski's.

I escaped their glow and navigated my way across the polished cement floor toward the stairs. I passed through a haphazard collection of heavy, clanking gym equipment, all in use by sweating men and women in gym clothes, towels around their shoulders, plastic water bottles by their sides. I went up the stairs, found room 202 and knocked. A muffled voice from inside invited me in.

Cochran was sitting on a bench on one side of the room with a small barbell in each hand. I watched him finish his curls. After a few seconds he put down the weights and wiped his face and hands with a towel.

"Greg! It's great to see you. Thanks for helping me with this. I couldn't think of anyone else who could do it." We shook hands.

Cochran, as I should have expected, was dressed in clothes suitable for exercising, sweatpants and a t-shirt. Still, his appearance took me by surprise, as it was the first time I'd seen him in anything other than a conservative business suit. Without it he didn't look like the squeaky-clean FBI agent I knew him to be. His blond hair was longer than it had been the last time I saw him, not well trimmed, and he needed a shave. Cochran saw me looking him over and laughed.

"Kind of a change, isn't it?" He held up a finger, then crossed to the door and opened it, peered out and closed it again.

He turned back to me with an embarrassed smile. "I know, it seems silly, but I've been building up an undercover identity for the past four months, and I have to be careful not to blow it." He motioned to a chair in the corner of the small room. I sat down, and he sat back on the weight bench. "Did Talbot explain what we're trying to do?"

"Not exactly, just some nonsense about a data card in a wallet."

Cochran gave a short laugh. That laugh told me all I needed to know as to how he felt about his new boss. "Yes, that sounds like Mister Special Agent Talbot. Everything on a need-to -know basis, and apparently only he needs to know."

"He told me Riley is back east teaching a course." The news of this had surprised me. "He made it sound like Riley was in the doghouse."

Cochran made a face. "That's his assignment. Two hours a day teaching a class on the fundamentals of investigations, and nothing to do the rest of the time. He's too senior, and he's cracked too many big cases to be forced out of the Bureau, but they can make him miserable enough to quit. I'm afraid that my boss—my old boss, that is—stepped on too many toes."

That wasn't difficult to believe. Riley had pulled all kinds of strings and bent quite a few corners getting me a clean record. Of course, I like to think I earned it. I started to ask Cochran more about what happened to Riley, but the uncomfortable look on his face caused me to decide to wait until later. I changed the subject to the matter at hand.

"So what is the story? What are you and Talbot up to, and what am I doing here?"

Cochran leaned back against the wall. "Ever hear of a guy named John Wolfe?"

I searched my memory. "He's that financier who ran away to the Cayman Islands or someplace like that. Looted his bank and got away with millions."

"It's closer to a billion, but that's about right. He loaded the bank up with sub-prime mortgages and sold them off to other banks. Lots of banks did that, but at least they kept a veneer of legality to it. Wolfe didn't bother. His outfit had teams of people faking documents and cooking the books. So far, twenty-seven people have been convicted of fraud, and some are getting serious jail time.

"But Wolfe got away."

"Yes, it's amazing what a few million in bribes will buy you. In his case it bought him a twenty-four hour warning, a home on a Caribbean island and a guarantee against extradition."

"Okay, that's who. What about why?"

Cochran chewed his lip. "I'm not certain how much I can tell you without the wrath of Talbot descending."

"He's that bad?"

"It's like he's looking for a reason to write me up. Kruger and Miss Yee have already jumped ship. They transferred together to another team down in LA."

Agents Kruger and Yee comprised the rest of the FBI team with whom I had worked last year.

"Okay, I won't press you, but you're going to have to give me details about the actual operation. I need to know as much as possible about who you are targeting and what the physical set-up will be."

"Do you really think you can teach me to lift a wallet without being caught?"

"Talbot tells me we have a month. I don't see why not, but it depends on the set-up, so give."

Cochran took a breath and dove into the story. "The target works for Wolfe. He's a trusted aide who hasn't been indicted yet, so he's able to fly into the city once a month from that island in the Caribbean. Wolfe is smart. He doesn't use email or call anyone on the telephone, so there's no way to set up a tap. Instead, he relies on this courier to carry those data cards."

"Who does he take them to?"

"Wolfe still controls a network of interlocking corporations here in the States. The courier takes the data card to Wolfe's stateside lawyer, and he distributes them. We believe those cards contain enough information for us to indict and extradite Wolfe."

I started to ask why Talbot didn't simply arrest Wolfe's lawyer, but Cochran was ahead of me. "Per Talbot, the lawyer, a guy named Dennis Metcalf, is off limits for us. Talbot says he doesn't want to contaminate the investigation by violating lawyer-client confidentiality. So that leaves the courier as the only avenue for us to get the data card. It's going to be tricky. The courier doesn't take a cab from the airport. He uses a private limo service. The same car and driver picks him up at the hotel in the morning, and he goes about whatever tasks Wolfe has assigned for him."

"How confident are you that the card will be in the courier's wallet?"

"Talbot is one hundred percent certain."

"And you?"

"Whoever it is that he's got working as a mole inside Wolfe's organization is close enough to the inner operation that his info is good."

Cochran took a drink from his water bottle and then continued. "We're thinking we can lift his wallet as he leaves his hotel, before he gets into the limo. The thing is," he leaned toward me, "it's critical to our plan that both the courier and Wolfe are confident the wallet was stolen by a street thief wanting a wallet, not by someone like us after the data card."

He gestured to his unkempt hair and the stubble on his face. "That's why I've been undercover the past few months. I've been building an identity as a small-time sneak thief. If Wolfe's people start checking things out, there will be enough people around who will identify me as such." He gave a slight smile. "Of course, I'll have to keep low afterwards. Wolfe is known to play for keeps."

I studied him anew. "Cochran, you have a devious mind. Now what do you say we get to work?"

I began by showing Cochran the basic concepts of picking pockets, using the same words that Fast Eddie had used all those years ago.

"It's all about misdirection. You have to give the mark something else to notice. That can be bumping into them, a loud noise, a pretty girl, a couple of people getting into a shouting match. Watch, the first time I saw Fast Eddie in action, this is what he did." I got down on one knee and pretended to tie my shoe.

"Then, when the mark is next to you," I stood up. "You bump into them and in the process take his wallet."

"Is that what you suggest I do?"

"No, there's too much chance of missing him if he veers around you. That's no problem when you're targeting strangers, but it won't work for you."

"So?"

I took off my coat. It was the same sports coat I'd practiced with the day before. I handed it to Cochran. "Here, put this on." He did.

"Does it fit?" I pulled the shoulders tight and straightened the lapels, moving around him like a tailor fitting a customer.

"Pretty much." Cochran seemed amused by my activity. I stepped back.

"Did you see what I was doing?"

"Not really. What were you doing?"

I held out my hand. There was a slim billfold in it. I held out my other hand. A silver pen and matching mechanical pencil were in it. Understanding dawned in Cochran's eyes.

"Those were in the coat, and you took them from me while you were moving around me."

I put the matching pen and pencil back into the jacket but kept the billfold. "Yes. Of course, I had the advantage of knowing where they were. That's really the first step. There are even ways of getting the mark to show you himself. It's pretty hard to steal something if you don't know where it is."

"Our man carries his wallet in the left inside pocket of his coat."

"Don't tell me, Talbot's pet mole again?"

"Who else?"

"Okay," I said. "That makes it easier already. Let's try that." I put the wallet back into the coat pocket on the left side, placing Cochran's hand on the breast of the coat so that he could feel the wallet and confirm that it was in place. "Now watch what I do."

I went through the motions again of adjusting the coat, walking around him and touching and pulling. Cochran's eyes followed my hands carefully. As I began tugging at the lapels, he grabbed my left hand. "There! You've got it in your hand now."

I slowly opened my fingers and showed him that they were empty. He checked my right hand but could see that it was empty, too. Cochran felt for the wallet through his coat. "But it's not there. You have it, don't you?"

I smiled and reached into my back pocket. I handed him the wallet. "I cheated," I admitted. "I never put it back in, only made it seem that way."

"But I felt it."

"You felt it, but I had my fingers inside the jacket and was holding it in place. As soon as you felt it and confirmed that it was back in the pocket, I let it drop down and caught it with my other hand."

Cochran shook his head. "I don't think I'm ever going to learn to do this."

I gave him a comforting pat on his shoulder. "Don't worry, Cochran. I'll make a thief of you yet."

Six

"Oh, no. This won't do at all."

The words woke me from my thoughts. I blinked and focused on the here and now.

It was the middle of the afternoon, and I was comfortably installed on the barstool behind the counter in the bookstore. My mind had been working the puzzle of how to teach Cochran the ancient art of picking pockets in only four weeks. I put down the pencil I twirled idly in my fingers and gave my attention to the young woman who stood in front of me

I hadn't taken much note of her when she'd walked into the store a few minutes earlier. I like to let customers explore the store on their own. I try not to bother them until they have a question. The woman was in her mid-twenties, short and slim, dressed in a business suit, the severe cut of which was offset by the small rectangular-framed glasses she wore and her high-heeled boots. Hairpins held long, reddish-dark hair in a tight bun in which I could see streaks of purple hiding. She had the look of a recent college graduate trying to look businesslike. I've found such people generally eschew any offers of help, having learned everything already.

Now, with her standing a scant two feet away, drumming her manicured fingernails on the counter, I figured it was possible I might have been wrong, though the small holes in her ears where multiple piercings had resided until recently suggested otherwise.

"I'm sorry if this," I motioned to the interior of The Book Nook, crammed from top to bottom with books, "won't do at all. Most of our customers seem to like it, though."

She placed a business card on the counter with a snap. "My name is April Quist, and I'm with Dunham Press. If you don't mind, I need to speak to the owner of this store."

I picked up the card and studied it with unhurried and exaggerated care. "April Quist, Author Event Coordinator." Her name and the publisher sounded familiar. A small poster taped to the side of our ancient cash register caught my eye. It advertised the upcoming reading and book signing by Max Carson. At the bottom of the poster was the name of Carson's publisher, Dunham Press.

"Oh, right, the book signing." What with Cochran, Talbot and everything in between, the book signing on Friday night had slipped my mind. It was four days away. "So tell me, Miss Quist, to what specifically are you referring when you say it won't do?"

"This whole place." She swept her arm around. "I mean, look at it. It's small, it's cramped, and there are only a couple of chairs. When Max Carson has a book signing, he draws crowds. This place is totally inadequate." She locked eyes with me as though daring me to challenge her. I accepted her dare.

"Miss Quist, if you had been a little more careful in your appraisal of my bookstore," I made certain to emphasize the fact that the store was mine, "you would have noticed that the bookshelves in the middle of the store are on wheels. We move them to the back room when we host events. Second, if you had bothered to ask, I would have told you that we have twenty-five folding chairs, more if needed, coming over from St. Timothy's down the street." She started to protest, but I raised my hand. "Finally, if your firm would like to cancel the book signing, that's fine with me. We'll simply send back all the copies of Max Carson's book that we ordered." I pointed to the display behind her. "It's completely up to you."

Miss Quist studied the display. It was stacked with hardcover editions of Max Carson's epic new novel, *Death & Deception at Donner Pass*. Her face grew pale, and she gulped. "No, I'm certain we can work with you on this to make it a success." She gave me a tentative smile. "I'm sorry if I was a bit of a bitch. Working for Max can do that. Actually, this is my first assignment. I only started with Dunham a month ago."

I did another quick calculation. "Let me guess, you graduated with your MFA this past June?"

She nodded.

"City College of Arts?"

She smiled and nodded again. "Yes. I'm lucky I found this job so quickly. Most of my class is still looking." Miss Quist lowered her voice as though imparting a book industry secret. "Though I'm beginning to suspect that the reason the job was open is because Max is such a pill to work for. He calls me at least five times a day."

A buzzing sound came from her Klug purse, an attractive, though modestly priced, style. It's not that I'm into fashion, but in my former line of work it was important for me to know what kind of clasps and fasteners different brands of purses used, and the best ways to open them without being noticed. The Klug line, though stylish, was child's play. Miss Quist took out a cell phone, and walked a few steps away from the counter.

"Yes, Max, what do you need?" She listened. "Yes, I'm at The Book Nook now, talking with the owner." The tone of her voice was like that of an adult to a troublesome child. "Yes, it looks like everything is fine. Yes, I understand. No, I haven't, but I'm still working on that. I will. Goodbye, Max." She returned to the counter.

"You see what I mean?" She gestured with the cell phone. "I had no idea a successful writer like Max Carson could be so insecure." She returned the cell phone to her purse and glanced at her watch.

"Darn. I need to run. If it's okay with you, I'll stop in again tomorrow afternoon to go over the details? I need to find Max a hotel room. The one I booked for him isn't up to his standards."

"Is he already in town?"

"No, not until Thursday, but apparently he looked up reviews of the hotel on the itinerary I sent him and decided it wasn't good enough." She sighed. "Nothing I studied in grad school covered the care and feeding of temperamental authors."

"You might have trouble finding something at this late date. There are several conventions in town."

She headed for the door, unsteady in her high-heeled boots. I figured she was still trying to make the transition from comfortable college clothes to dress-for-success attire. She clopped her way to the front door. "Then I'd better get hustling. See you tomorrow afternoon."

Seven

A little bell on a thread jingled, and that tiny sound caused me to sigh. "Try again."

Cochran walked away from me, reached the wall and turned. He must have been as tired as I was of this exercise, but he made up in determination what he lacked in dexterity. "Let's go," he said, game as ever.

I turned away from him and stood with a newspaper in front of me, pretending to be engrossed in the sports scores. Cochran appeared next to me on my left. With my peripheral vision I could see that he, too, was holding a newspaper. His paper was folded, and he held it with both hands. He gave the paper a shake and flipped it over the way commuters do, with practiced, bored movements. So far, so good. The next few seconds would tell.

That damned little bell gave out its musical tinkle again. It was Cochran's turn to sigh.

"Darn, I thought I had it that time."

I put my hand inside my coat. My billfold was halfway out of the inside pocket. "What happened?" I put it back in place and faced Cochran.

"I had it in the scissors grasp, but it slipped sidewise as I pulled it out."

I held my coat open. "Show me."

Cochran reached with his left hand and dipped into the coat pocket. He began drawing my billfold out and, just as he said, halfway out it slipped and turned within his fingers. The little bell, one of many suspended by tiny threads across the inside of my jacket, tinkled as the slim wallet brushed against it.

"Okay, I think I see the problem." My hand replaced his. "Watch my hand," I commanded.

I slid my hand sideways into my coat pocket, and keeping my fingers straight and stiff, took hold of the billfold by slipping it between my index and ring fingers. "Now, watch, see how I lift it straight up and how well I've got hold of it. It takes the full length of your fingers to hold it. You have to account for the depth of the jacket pocket. The average suit coat inside pocket is at least six inches deep." I pulled the billfold all the way out. No bells tinkled. "See, no movement to give you away."

Cochran dutifully nodded.

"Let's take a break," I suggested. We went over to a couple of chairs by the wall and sat down, both of us extending our legs out straight.

We'd been at it for over an hour that morning, the fourth day of my tutorial for Cochran on the fine and ancient art of pickpocketing. I wish I could say I was encouraged by his progress, but I wasn't. The small exercise room upstairs at Wykowski's Gym had no windows, and the air was stuffy. An overhead fluorescent fixture washed everything in a sterile light. The smell of decades of sweat had permeated the walls, ceiling and floor.

The bells were my latest effort and illustrated how frustrated I'd become. I'm not a graduate of The School of Seven Bells, nor have I ever met anyone who was, or at least admitted to it. It's a legendary school for pickpockets located somewhere high in the Andes Mountains in South America. Heck, I'm not even certain that it still exists, if it ever really did. Still, most of us in the pickpocketing business know about it and the techniques said to be taught there, first and foremost of which is the use of little bells on strings. Students are tested on their ability to slip a wallet out of a pocket without causing a bell to ring.

"I'm not picking it up very fast, am I?"

I could hear the discouragement in his voice. "No," I admitted, "you aren't, but we have three weeks to go, so let's not give up yet."

"I won't, but I'm going to have to warn Talbot that we'll need a backup plan if I'm not ready in time."

I wondered what kind of plan that would be. Whatever it was, I was determined to have nothing to do with it.

"You know, Greg, you're a dying breed."

"Gee, thanks."

"I don't mean any offense, but it's a simple fact. Pickpockets are disappearing from the US crime scene."

"How do you mean?" I have to admit, loner that I am, I never paid much attention to how many of my brethren there were. My former brethren, that is.

"Over the past twenty years the number of pickpockets working the streets has dropped by seventy percent, at least based on arrest stats. People don't carry as much cash as they used to."

"Yes, but the credit cards are still worth something."

"You have to have a good fence for those."

I thought back to my old fence, Sammie the Louse. "You have a point," I conceded.

"And another thing, there's no next generation of pickpockets. The young street kids aren't interested in spending the hundreds of hours you did learning the trade. Instead, they prefer to stick people up with a knife or a gun or grab a purse and run. The old techniques are disappearing. In a few years almost no one will know how to do what you do."

I laughed. "Gee, Cochran, you sound almost nostalgic for my old and wicked, wicked ways."

He smiled. "No, at least don't let Talbot get that idea. But …" he grew silent.

"But?"

"Ask any cop on the street in a large city, and they'll tell you they miss the days of the nonviolent sneak thief. There was a certain mutual respect between cop and pickpocket years ago, and that's pretty much gone now."

"Guess it's good I got out when I did."

"Yeah, I'd have to agree."

I checked the clock on the wall. "Speaking of which, I'd better get going. Miss Quist is dropping by again this afternoon."

"Max Carson's advance woman?" I'd told Cochran about our upcoming big author event and how Miss April Quist was fixating on every detail prior to the arrival of the Big Author himself.

"Yep. Today she wants to go over to St. Timothy's to check the quality of the folding chairs they are lending us." I got up. Cochran did so, as well, but put out a hand as I turned to leave.

"Before you go, take a look at these photos, will you?" He reached into his coat and brought out a small envelope. He opened it and removed several small photos and gave them to me. "This is Zager, the courier whose pocket I have to pick."

I studied the photos. There were three, each showing the same man. The first caught him as he approached the photographer, the second as he passed. The third photo showed Zager standing on a sidewalk, talking with another man. Zager was of medium height, medium build, with medium length hair and a face that most people would forget five minutes after meeting him. It was the perfect combination for a courier of clandestine content.

The man he was talking with was the physical opposite of Zager. He was tall, with a lean, aristocratic face. From his and Zager's postures there was no doubt of who was the master and who was the servant.

"Is this John Wolfe?" I asked, pointing to the other man.

Cochran shook his head. "No, that's Dennis Metcalf, Wolfe's lawyer here in the states."

"This is the guy your boss says is off limits?"

"That's right. I suggested that I could go and interview him, just for background information, a few weeks back, but Talbot turned me down." He reached for the photographs.

I took a last look at the photos before handing them back. Something had caught my eye. I scanned each again. I tapped the first photo, the one showing Zager walking toward the camera. "See this guy?" I pointed to a man trailing Zager.

"That's a local hood," answered Cochran. "Strictly muscle, hired to provide a little added protection. Why?"

"I know him. His name is," I searched my memory. I only thought of him, when I thought of him at all, as Donnie's guy. "His name is Joey. He works for Donnie at the Pink Poodle."

"Used to work for him. Now he works for Dominic DeMarco. DeMarco runs a sort of rent-a-tough operation for people visiting from out of town."

I shook my head. "Well, I hope they're not paying too much for Joey. He's not exactly top of the line in the smarts department."

Soon after that we parted ways, Cochran to head back to the undercover life he was living and me to what I thought of as my real life. The life where I have a wife, a bookstore, an anal-retentive author's public relations woman hounding me about folding chairs, and only a distant memory of being a pickpocket.

Eight

"Next week? That's impossible!" I slammed my hand on the table. The plastic tumblers of ice water jumped. Talbot reached over and moved them closer to where he sat opposite me. He glanced from left to right, but the tables on either side of us in the little diner were empty.

"Mr. Smith, why don't we let Agent Cochran say whether or not he thinks he's ready?" I looked over at Cochran sitting at my side. He was trying to flip a spoon between his fingers the way I taught him. Just then the spoon slipped out of his grasp and clattered to the tabletop. He made a face and shook his head.

"Greg's right, Talbot. There's no way I can be ready by next week. Heck, I don't know if I'll ever get the hang of it. We need to develop an alternative plan."

The waitress came over with our coffees, and we stopped talking as she placed them on the table along with a small bowl of creamer packets and a wicker basket filled with real and artificial sugar packets. I picked up my coffee and took a sip. It was dark and bitter, just like my mood.

Late Friday morning Cochran and I had finished our session at the gym when his cell phone rang. It was Talbot, asking the two of us to meet him at a diner down the street. That's where he dropped the bombshell on us. The plans had changed. Zager, the courier whose pocket it was so important for Cochran to pick, was arriving on Wednesday of next week, not three weeks later.

"There," I said to Talbot. "Cochran agrees with me. You'll just have to find a different plan."

Talbot leaned back. "I'm sorry to hear that. Having Agent Cochran perform the task would have been preferable, but we'll simply have to have someone else do it."

A chill came over me. "Wait a minute, Talbot."

"Yes, Mr. Smith?" The bastard's smooth voice matched his face.

"You are not getting me to do it." I stabbed my finger on the table with each word. "There is no way I'm getting involved in your scheme."

"Well, let's see about that, shall we?" Talbot opened a portfolio, withdrew an envelope and placed it on the table in front of him.

Cochran lifted his hands in protest. "Don't look at me, Greg. I have no idea what he's up to."

I turned back to Talbot. He smiled and slipped a paper folded lengthwise part way from the envelope. The paper was a heavy stock, and there was large printing near the top that read Arrest Warrant.

I leaned back and shook my head. "No. No way. You can't arrest me. I have a clean record. Riley arranged it. You tried this before, remember?" I turned to Cochran. "I don't know how you ended up working for this guy, Cochran, but I feel sorry for you. He doesn't seem to catch on too well." I started to get up.

"Sit down, Mister Smith." Talbot's voice cut like a knife. "Your guilty conscience is causing you to jump to conclusions. This warrant isn't for you."

I sat back down. I was starting to get a very bad feeling about what was coming. "Then who is it for?"

"It's for a friend of yours, a very close friend." He drew the rest of the warrant from the envelope, and I saw the name on it. It was Barbara's.

Nine

Cochran and I didn't talk as he drove us back to The Book Nook. I think he was too embarrassed, and I was too furious. We parked in a lot off Knickerbocker Lane and walked the few blocks to the store. The bell jangled as we pushed through the front door.

Tom was behind the counter. He called hello and then a friendly greeting when he recognized Cochran. Cochran walked over to shake hands. Poor Junior meowed a greeting to me, but I ignored him and went on into the back room, making the beaded curtain swirl and clack wildly in my wake.

Barbara was stirring something that boiled and bubbled in an old stockpot. "Hi, Greg, you're just in time to taste this." She walked over with a wooden spoon and held it up.

I watched her face as she caught sight of the look on mine.

"Greg, what's the matter?" She carried the spoon back to the pot and wiped her hands on her apron. I heard soft footsteps behind me. It was Lynn coming down from the dance studio.

I looked at both of them. "Good, I'm glad you're here. We need to talk."

The next minute found the four of us seated at the table in the back room kitchen of The Book Nook. Barbara and Lynn were surprised to see Cochran, but my evident sour mood gave them warning that this was not a social call.

"Here's the deal," I said, cutting to the chase. "Talbot's little operation has hit a snag. The dip has to be performed next week, not in three weeks, and there's no way Cochran can be ready."

Cochran lifted his hands. "I'm trying, but Greg's right."

"So?" Lynn asked.

I looked straight in her eyes and took her hand in mine. "So Talbot wants me to do it."

Lynn snatched her hand away. "Greg! You promised."

I took her hand again, holding it against her attempt to take it away. "That's right, I promised. Only guess what?" I looked around the table from Lynn to Barbara to Cochran.

"What?" Lynn's voice was defeated. I was failing her, and we both knew it.

"Only if I don't go through with it, he's arresting Barbara on a charge of aiding and abetting the escape of a man wanted for blowing up a bank and killing the night watchman."

Lynn laughed. "That's ridiculous, Greg. Barbara? For a moment I thought you were serious."

The three of us didn't say anything. Lynn searched my face, then Cochran's, and then—reluctantly, as though she would see an answer she didn't want to see—Barbara's.

Barbara sighed and shook her head. "It's Jimmie LeCuyer, isn't it?"

Cochran nodded.

"My goodness," said Barbara. "There's a name from the past. I haven't thought about Jimmie in years, decades."

"I don't understand," asked Lynn. "Who is Jimmie LeCuyer?"

"Go ahead, Agent Cochran," said Barbara. "Tell her."

Cochran related the story Talbot had told me only an hour before. It was about James LeCuyer, a leader of the radical black student movement back in the late 1960s. LeCuyer had decided to finance the revolution by blowing the door off a bank vault in the middle of the night. This was in Madison, where he was a student at the University of Wisconsin. He got away with over half a million dollars in cash, but a night watchman's body was later found in the rubble. LeCuyer sent a letter to the newspapers, saying he was sorry for the guard's death and explaining he didn't know the man was in the building. James LeCuyer then went underground and evaded a nationwide manhunt. In 1970 he was spotted in Cuba as an honored guest of Fidel. When last heard of, he was teaching political science at the University of Havana.

"There's no statute of limitations on murder," concluded Cochran, "and anyone who helped LeCuyer in his escape could still be prosecuted."

He stood up. "At this time I think I'd better leave. I don't want to hear anything I would have to report."

Barbara reached over and took his hands in hers. "You'll come back a little later for lunch? I've made soup."

He gave a slight smile. "Thank you. I'll come back if I can." Cochran then turned to Lynn. "It's nice to see you again, Lynn. I only wish it was under better circumstances."

Lynn gave him a half-smile. We waited until Cochran left the back room and we heard the front door bell before anyone spoke again.

It was Barbara who went first. "I knew Jimmie, of course. I knew everyone in the protest movements back then. He stayed here a number of times, and if he stayed here while he was on the run, well, it's possible. I didn't ask questions of those who stayed here."

"That's not much reason to arrest Barbara," Lynn said to me. "Don't you think Talbot is just bluffing? There isn't a juror in the state who would convict her almost fifty years later."

"Actually, Talbot agrees," I admitted. "He said as much. He also pointed out how it would take a year or two to fight this in court and an awful lot of money, money none of us have." There was silence again. I hated having to bring up Talbot's other threat, but I had to. "Then there's the store."

"The Book Nook?" Lynn and Barbara spoke at once.

"What about it?" asked Barbara. "You and Lynn own it now, not me."

"Yes, but how did you pay for everything when you started it? Can you prove that none of the missing bank money was used to buy this building back then? It's about the same time you bought it, isn't it?"

Barbara's face grew pale.

"Prove it? Of course I can't prove anything after all these years." She let out an anguished cry. "Oh, Greg, could they really take The Book Nook from you?"

"Talbot thinks so," I said. "He says it's covered under ill-gotten gains. Again, we could fight it in court, but in the meantime the store would be closed. They could even sell our inventory and take that money."

"I don't think I like Mr. Talbot very much," said Barbara.

"It's okay," I told her. "I'll do this for him, and then we'll be free of him forever."

Barbara shook her head and got up from the table. She looked older and sadder than I had ever seen her. Her eyes were wet.

"If you'll excuse me, I'm going to go lie down for a while." She left the kitchen and went into her bedroom. The door shut behind her.

I saw Lynn studying my face. "That's not all, is it, Greg?"

"It's worse," I admitted. "Cochran has spent the last four months building up a reputation as a sneak thief, because the only way this gambit is going to work is if Wolfe and his people believe the wallet was stolen by someone who didn't know what was in it."

"So Cochran's been out there stealing stuff? How can the police allow this?"

"The police know nothing about it. Also, Cochran has been delivering what he steals to a tame fence the feds have. Eventually what he steals ends up back with the person he stole it from." I didn't mention it, but I knew who the tame fence was.

It didn't take Lynn long to realize where all this was heading. "Greg, does that mean you have to go back to picking pockets?"

"It's the only way to do it. I'll start on Monday."

Lynn tried to object but I cut her off. "Lynn, too many people know that I gave it up. If this is going to work everyone has to believe I've taken it up again."

"Everyone?"

"You, Barbara, Cochran, Talbot and their tame fence will be the only ones who know the truth."

"That means you could be picked up by the police, doesn't it?"

"Yes."

In the end there was no other conclusion. We were screwed, and I was going to have to do what Talbot wanted me to do. I pushed my cell phone over to Lynn. "I told Talbot I'd send him a text message if I agreed."

"When you agreed, you mean." Lynn's eyes blazed with a cold anger. "I hate Talbot, and I hate what he's forcing you to do."

"You send the message," I told her.

She picked up the phone and retrieved Talbot's number. "What should I say?"

"Whatever you like. If you don't want me to do it, then tell him the deal is off."

Lynn looked over at the closed door of Barbara's room.

"We don't have a choice, do we?"

I shook my head. Lynn pressed a few buttons, then a last one—the send button. She handed the phone back to me, and I read the message she sent. It was short and not very sweet.

"The Kid is back."

Ten

Max Carson strode into The Book Nook like a western gunslinger entering a saloon. He wore a tan leather duster that came down past his knees, but not so far as to keep his hand-tooled, snakeskin boots from view. His cowboy hat showed enough wear to appear authentic, but not so much as to obscure its expert craftsmanship. His face was tanned and his hair was an impressive mane, mostly black, shot through with the right amount of gray to impart gravitas, but not enough to be called grizzled.

He stood for a moment just inside the doorway, looking the place over as though half-expecting someone to make the mistake of challenging him. Behind him I could see the slight form of April Quist, flitting like a butterfly from side to side, trying to squeeze past the great author. Finally she ducked under his arm and slipped inside the store. She tottered in her high-heeled boots over to the counter and stuck out her hand. Just as I reached out my own hand, the strap of her heavy purse slipped from her shoulder to her elbow, pulling her arm down.

"Oh, jeez, I'm sorry," she said as she pulled her purse strap back onto her shoulder, took a moment to push her glasses back up on her nose and put out her hand again. This time I was able to reach it. No sooner had she shaken my hand than she dropped it, turned and swept her arm toward the door. "Greg Smith, I'd like to introduce Max Carson." Her purse slid down her arm again, spoiling the effect.

An awkward moment followed. It was clear that Max Carson expected me to come over to him, but I was behind the counter and didn't see any reason to act deferential.

Miss Quist was at a loss as to what to do. Her eyes lit on the display of Max's new novel. "Max, come and see this wonderful display," she said.

He ambled over, stopping a few feet short of the counter. Miss Quist's eyes caught mine, and I could read her silent plea. Oh, what the heck, I figured. If Max could go halfway, I could, too, and walked out from behind the counter and offered my hand to our visitor.

Max shook it with gusto. "Nice to meet you, young fellow. Nice to meet you." His eyes lifted as he looked over my shoulder.

I turned and saw Barbara and Lynn slipping through the beaded curtain from the back room. Barbara was dressed, as she was on most days, in a simple sundress that either copied the style of the sixties or actually dated to those years. Her long hair was braided around her head as usual. Lynn had probably just finished teaching a class, as she was wearing her dancer's leotard and soft shoes. Her long black hair was tied back in a severe ponytail.

Max's face broke into a smile worthy of a matinee idol. "And who are these lovely ladies?" He swept off his hat in an exaggerated bow.

I've no doubt there are women who enjoy such theatrics, but neither Barbara nor Lynn is among them. Barbara took her glasses from where they hung on a slender chain around her neck and put them on. She studied Max's face and compared it to the photograph of Max on the back of the many books on the display table.

"Mr. Carson? Welcome to our store."

I made the introductions.

I saw April Quist eyeing the clutter in the store. Folding chairs were stacked against the bookcases, and there was little floor space visible.

"We weren't expecting you until around six," I explained. "The event doesn't begin until seven, you know." I walked over to one of floor displays. "We're going to wheel these into the back room in a few minutes and then set up the chairs."

"Well, maybe I can lend a hand," said Max, and before I could say a word in protest, he shucked his coat and draped it over the counter. A second later his hat joined it.

Between the two of us we cleared the floor space in minutes and began setting up the chairs. Max took great delight in making as much noise as possible, clattering the metal chairs against each other as he positioned them, then repositioned them again and again. He noticed that I was watching him.

"When you've given as many of these little talks as I have, son, you understand how important it is to have the chairs in just the right spots."

He walked over to the front door, then turned and pointed at the first row of chairs. "You see? A person walking in is going to want to sit at the back. That's why we put only a couple of chairs near the door. We want them to have to come up close to where I'll be. That's how you get them to buy books."

Lynn and Miss Quist wheeled a small cart out from the back room. It held paper cups and would hold the coffee pot later. "No, no, not there," commanded Max. They had put the cart near the counter. He came over and wheeled the cart across the room. "Here," he announced. "You want people to have to walk past me to get to the coffee. They're much more likely to buy a copy of the book that way."

I began to realize that Max Carson, his cowboy persona aside, was keenly interested in selling as many copies of his book as possible.

The Book Nook was ready for the big event well before six o'clock. I tactfully suggested to Miss Quist that she could take Max down the street to a small Greek bistro and get him something to eat before we started. I was weary of Max Carson and welcomed the thought of an hour without him, but Max would have nothing of it.

"Nonsense, son." He took a deep breath. "The whole time I've been here I've been smelling soup, and in my not so humble opinion, home-made soup is the finest soup there is."

Barbara had come out from the back room just then. I watched the emotions cross her face. Max was a loud and boorish man, but he was a guest, and guests are sacred to Barbara. She smiled as her innate good nature won over.

"You are correct, Mister Carson. You do smell soup. It's beef and rice soup, and I made it just today. You are welcome to have some if you like."

Max slapped me on the back. "You see, son? Come on, let's go eat."

Max, April, Lynn, Barbara and I crowded around the table in the back room of the store. We've often had six or more people at that table, but Max's overlarge personality managed to make it feel crowded. I watched Barbara ladle the soup into bowls and wondered if there would be enough for everyone.

Much to my annoyance, Junior took a liking to Max and hopped onto his lap when he sat down at the table. Max earned a point in his favor by understanding that this was an honor. He rubbed Junior behind his ears for a few seconds and then went on eating. Junior blinked his eyes at me as though daring me to complain. I ignored the little traitor.

"So," said Lynn in an effort to start a conversation as we ate. "Mister Carson, I understand your book is about the Donner Party."

Max was offended. "You mean you haven't read it?"

Lynn shook her head. "No, I'm afraid I've been too busy."

Max placed his large hand over Lynn's. "That's okay, little lady. I'll make certain you get a signed copy with a personal dedication from me to you."

"Isn't that great, Lynn?" I asked with an innocent smile. Beneath the table her foot made sharp contact with my shin.

"Max's book is creating quite a stir," said April, properly playing the role of publicist. "In it, he shows how what happened to the Donner Party was the result of the theft of a US Cavalry payroll."

"That's hard to believe," said Barbara.

"No, not if you know as much about it as I do," said Max. "I believe that my novel, though presented as fiction, is the true story of what happened to those poor settlers."

"Fiddlesticks," said Barbara. "I've read the diaries of Tamzene Donner and Patricia Reed. There's no mention of such a thing in them."

"Exactly!" said Max with triumph. "That shows you how well the thieves covered their tracks."

Made mute by his ludicrous illogic, we could only stare back at him.

The bell above the shop door jingled. It was six-thirty. "I guess people are starting to arrive," I said, getting up from the table. "Max, why don't you stay and finish eating while Lynn and I take care of a few final things up front?"

Lynn and I made our escape as fast as we could. As I expected, the visitor was Old Tom. I told him there might be some soup left for him, and at the same time he could meet the great Max Carson. Tom went to the back room, leaving us alone.

"He'd better be worth this," Lynn said quietly to me as we stood in the bookstore surveying the scene. "If he calls me little lady again, he's going to regret it."

I told her how much the profit margin was on each of his books. She counted the number of chairs, did a quick calculation, and her eyebrows went up. "I suppose he's worth it."

Max chose just that moment to sweep through the bead curtain from the back room.

"Hey, little lady, I didn't get a chance to tell you the rest of that story."

Lynn punched me on the arm, stalked past Max and left without saying a word.

Max watched her leave, then turned back to me. "Kind of a moody girl, ain't she?"

I explained to Max that Lynn had a lot of prep work to do for her dancing classes.

He studied the poster on the wall. "Adult dancing?" he asked. "Is that what I think it is?"

He didn't give me a chance to answer as he smiled a lecherous grin. "Well, what do you know? I guess you bookstore types get to have a little fun after all, don't you?"

"Bookstore types?"

"Yeah, you know. You guys always have your noses in books. You read so much you miss what's going on in the real world."

He walked over to the front door and opened it with a flourish. He continued talking as the bell jangled an accompaniment. "Son, outside there's a whole world going on. There's action out on those streets you couldn't imagine in your wildest dreams."

"There is, is there?"

"There certainly is. Son, I could show you a side of life you don't know exists. It's my job as a writer to explore not just the best in people but the worst, as well. Why, you and I could walk down this street, and I could point out to you who's a saint and who's a sinner."

"Really?"

"You bet I could. Son, there are crooks out there who could steal you blind without you suspecting a thing. Why, I could …" His words were cut off as two people walked through the door he was holding open. Max Carson's audience was arriving.

Eleven

Max Carson may be a hack writer, and Lynn may add that he's a chauvinist of porcine parentage. Barbara may simply sniff and say he's a phony from his hat down. But after watching him in action at the book signing that evening, all three of us had to agree that Max Carson was also one heck of a showman.

He began the event by reading a short selection from his book, and he chose well. Some writers choose the first page or two of their novel. Some choose favorite passages, those they are proud of as a writer. Max was one of the comparatively few writers who know how to choose passages that hook the audience and make them want to buy the book. He picked a passage that began with these words:

"Theirs were the last covered wagons that summer to leave Independence, Missouri. They knew they needed to push hard to reach the Sierras before winter set in and made the passage impossible. Donner, the man elected by the other settlers as leader, relied on Reed's experience at traveling through rough terrain. Reed insisted that they make their way through the Wasatch Mountains to the Utah Territories via Hasting's Cutoff, as it promised to shave critical time and distance from their race against the coming snows. But the eighty-one people, including thirty-five children, soon found themselves struggling to travel through mountains where boulders blocked their way, and across deserts where sand mired their wheels. They were a month behind schedule by the time they reached Jim Bridger's trading post at the foot of the Sierras. What they didn't know was that taking that route was Reed's way to justify his rendezvous with Lanford Hastings at Bridger's. That is where the conspirators intended to transfer the stolen gold, and what those poor people didn't know was going to kill more than half of them and cause the memory of those who survived to live in infamy."

Max described the research he had conducted when preparing to write his book, how he had studied diaries, letters and other contemporary accounts. He talked about the trips he had taken, arduously retracing the settlers' route. April Quist passed around photos Max had taken when he'd visited the Alder Creek and Donner Lake where the Donner Party had spent that fateful winter. He held up a piece of a broken ceramic plate that he said he'd found there and, in his expert opinion, must have belonged to the settlers.

Max admitted he had no irrefutable proof to back his claim of stolen gold being secretly transported by the Donner Party, but I saw more than a few people in the audience nodding as he listed what he claimed were irrefutable pieces of evidence that supported his conjecture.

However, what regard Max had built up in me for him was tossed away by his answer to an innocuous question by a fan. "Mr. Carson," gushed a middle-aged woman with dyed hair and too much makeup, "I admire you so much. You go out and live your life to the fullest while the rest of us stay at home and only dream."

"Thank you, Ma'am," he answered. "Yes, I was just saying to young Greg over there," he pointed to where I was standing behind the counter. "I was just telling him that while he's lived his life inside of books, I've been outside in the real world living life as it really is."

I began to speculate about what would happen if Max were to find his wallet missing.

The question and answer portion of the evening went on for another fifteen minutes. The audience then dispersed to taste the snacks and drink the coffee we'd set out and buy autographed copies of Max's book. April took one photograph after another of Max with his fans.

At length the event was over. The chairs were folded and put on carts for rolling back to St. Timothy's in the morning. I made certain a signed copy of Max's book was placed with them for the rector. I know The Reverend Cathy Walton and also know of her love for westerns.

"So, son, I don't suppose you know a good place where a fella can get a decent drink around here, do you?" I started to answer, but Max cut me off. "No, that's okay. I've got a nose for such things." He placed one long finger against his nose. "I'm sure I can sniff one out quick enough." He turned to April, who was hovering nearby. "Come along, little lady. You and I are gonna' do the town."

April protested that they had an early morning guest spot on a local radio show, but Max would have none of it. They left with April trying to get Max to agree to just one drink before going back to the hotel.

I closed the door behind them, glad to be finished with the Great Max Carson.

Twelve

The woman standing next to me on the bus was an ideal target. She was talking on her cell phone, making plans for that evening, oblivious to what was going on around her. The bus was crowded enough that I was justified in standing only inches away.

I gave a quick glance to ensure no one was watching and let my arm drop to my side, next to her purse. My fingers worked the latch. I kept my eyes on the woman's face, watching to see if she noticed me opening her purse. She didn't. I reached into my own pants pocket and withdrew a business card and slipped it into her purse and then closed it again. At the next stop, I got off the bus.

The next time she looked in her purse, perhaps when putting her cell phone away, she would find my card. It's a simple card with a simple message, "Surprise! You've been put-pocketed!" In smaller letters at the bottom it says, "Courtesy of your friendly neighborhood pickpockets."

It was Saturday afternoon. Although I had told Lynn that I would start picking pockets on Monday, I decided to spend the weekend brushing up on my skills by engaging in some put-pocketing, picking pockets in reverse, so to speak.

I don't know who came up with the idea of it, but put-pocketing is a way for pickpockets to keep up their skills without having to worry too much about being arrested. It also serves as a warning to people to keep a better watch over their property.

I spent Saturday afternoon riding the streetcars and buses, slipping my cards into the purses and pockets of unwitting victims. I kept an eye out for people watching me, fellow practitioners taking note of a competitor, but couldn't tell if I was seen.

I spent Sunday afternoon at City Center where crowds of tourists filled the enormous expanse of concrete, replacing the office workers and other working stiffs of weekday afternoons. Sidewalk venders hawked their wares, street musicians competed with each other for volume and tips, and pigeons enjoyed the visitors' largesse. If I wanted word to spread on the street that I had returned to picking pockets, and I did, this was the place to do it. Over the afternoon I left a couple of dozen cards, and as I did I was aware of more than a few pairs of eyes watching me.

I paused for a moment outside a bookstore on the plaza. It's a local chain and well regarded, as they do a good job of promoting local authors. To my chagrin, there was a large display of Max Carson's book in the window with posters for a signing there by Max on Thursday evening. I remembered that April had mentioned Max was staying in town for ten days, working the bookstore circuit, giving interviews and making public appearances. His appearance at our store had been only a warm-up for the larger venues. I shook my head. There was just no escaping the guy.

As I studied the window display I became aware of someone standing about forty feet behind me. I could see him in the window's reflection. He was noticeable, as he was standing still while others walked past him. He was too far away for me to make out his face.

I turned halfway and began to walk across the plaza at an angle that let me keep my watcher visible in the corner of my eye without it being obvious I was aware of him. By the time I passed him I had a pretty good idea who it was—Chad, the pickpocket from the book fair. Well, I wanted word to get out that I had returned to the street, and now I knew that Doris Whitaker would hear of it soon.

Mission accomplished, I headed back to The Book Nook.

Thirteen

"Hey, Kid, good to see you. I heard you were back working the street."

"Hello, Jay, long time no see." We shook hands. Jay motioned in the direction of some shade by the side of a nearby building, and we walked a few steps over to its shelter. We leaned our backs against the wall, talking sideways to each other. Pedestrians streamed by on the busy downtown sidewalk.

Jay was a street fence, someone who buys and sells stolen credit cards and such from people like me on the street.

It was mid-morning on Tuesday, the second day of my return to a life of crime. In the last twenty-four hours I had relieved a couple of dozen people of their wallets and gleaned a handful of watches from their owners. I tried to target people who could get along without those items for a few days until the feds quietly returned them as found property. That didn't mean I felt good about it.

"How's Lynn and married life?" Jay asked.

"Lynn's fine," I answered. "How's Dave?" Dave is Jay's partner and runs a small dog grooming business.

"Dave's fine. The shop's keeping him pretty busy these days. I've been helping out when I can." The edges of his mouth dropped. "I might as well. It's getting harder and harder to work the street."

"How so?"

"Doris Whitaker is making a heavy play to take charge of pickpocketing in the city. She's dictating who works where and what we fences can charge."

I made a note of that.

Jay surveyed the crowd. "So if you're back in business, Kid, where are you dropping your merchandise? I'm always willing to deal with you, you know."

"Here and there," I answered. I didn't want to bring too much scrutiny to the fed's tame fence. Plus, I had to keep up appearances. "What are you looking for?"

"The usual. Credit cards, gift cards, driver's licenses. There's a couple of outfits from out of town, Russian, I think, that are buying them up as quick as they can."

I nodded. "I'll keep that in mind."

We chatted a few more minutes and then shook hands. Jay left, and after a moment I did the same.

I was half a block down the street from the federal building. I liked the idea of targeting fellow employees of the man who was forcing me back to working the street.

I spotted a likely mark after a couple of minutes.

The man wore a nice suit and was walking toward me, perhaps forty feet away and closing fast. He held a cell phone to his ear. Just what the doctor ordered. When a person is talking on a cell phone, fully fifty percent of his attention is on the person at the other end of the connection, making it much easier for me. I made a subtle correction to the course my feet were taking and brushed against the man as we passed.

"Sorry," I said as I recovered from a near fall, then continued on my way, his wallet tucked up my sleeve. When he noticed it missing, he would probably have no memory of my bumping into him, let alone be able to describe me.

I still had an hour to kill before I was due to meet my fence, and to tell the truth I was getting bored. I decided to ratchet things up a notch. I searched the plaza and spotted a man and woman walking together. Both carried slim attaché cases and wore conservative business suits. They were talking to each other in an animated fashion as they walked. I walked straight toward them, a wide smile filling my innocent face.

"Glenn? Glenn Raeder? How the heck are you?" The man's surprise was obvious as I shook his hand.

"No," he protested. "No, that's not my name. You have me confused with someone else." The woman watched with amusement.

I turned to her in appeal. "Glenn's always doing that, always pretending to be someone else, especially when he's with a beautiful woman who's not his wife."

Her smile became a laugh. "Sorry, but he really isn't Glenn Raeder. His name is Tom. Tom Driscol."

I feigned incredulity.

"Not Glenn?" I stood back a step, and took his left hand by the wrist and held his arm out as though examining him. In reality I was slipping my index finger between the tail of his watchband and the clasp and pushing it back through. In a second I had it free. I dropped his wrist.

"Wow, I am sorry," I said to the man, then to the woman. "He's the spitting image of someone I went to school with." I named the school, a prestigious law school on the other side of the country.

The woman smiled again, clearly amused by her colleague's predicament. "That's quite all right."

The two walked away, and I melted back into the crowd, the man's watch safely in my pocket.

It was time to go see my favorite fence.

Fourteen

Sammie the Louse was the only fence I'd trusted back when I worked the streets. I took the 51 bus from downtown toward the old Tenderloin District. Once there, I walked a couple of quick blocks along cracked sidewalks and past derelict shops and businesses where once bright windows were now protected by iron bars, and doors had steel shutters that rolled down at night. Even in the middle of the day the air stank of decay and neglect. I'm no fan of urban renewal, but if ever a neighborhood qualified as being blighted, the Tenderloin was it.

I reached Sammie's storefront and pushed open the door. Although it had been over a year since I last visited, the place was still the same. Faded cardboard containers cluttered the shelves along with a bewildering assortment of old toasters, radios, phonograph players and the like. A thin sheen of dust lay on all the exposed flat surfaces.

The floor creaked as I walked up to the gated sales counter. The girl behind the counter, Sammie's daughter, looked up from her book. Her eyes, thick with mascara and eye shadow, widened as she recognized me.

"Hello Mary."

She nodded in return. Still as talkative as ever.

I stole a look at the book she was reading. *Siddhartha*, by Herman Hesse. "Moved on from existentialism, I see."

Her eyes flickered to the book and back to me. "I guess you want to see my dad."

It was my turn to nod.

She pressed a button with her foot, and there was a soft click from the shelves to my left. I went over to them and pulled. The wall, complete with shelves full of merchandise, swung open silently, and I stepped through. I sensed rather than heard the secret door close behind me.

"Kid! Right on time." Sammie got up from his desk and came toward me.

"Hello, Sammie," I answered. "I have to admit I didn't expect to find myself here again."

"Yeah, life can take some strange turns, ain't that the truth." Sammie went back to his desk.

I watched him, overcome by déjà vu. How many times before had I arrived here with stolen wallets and watches to sell? How many times had Sammie sat behind that desk as he was now, waiting for me to pour out the contents of my pockets?

Everything was the same and yet at the same time, everything was different. In a rundown building in a rundown neighborhood, Sammie's office was an oasis of taste. The carpet was both expensive and tasteful. The lighting was subdued and brought out the richness of the wood paneling. A Julie London recording played softly on hidden speakers.

Short and round-faced, Sammie looked at me with an open honesty that belied his occupation. Everything was as it used to be except for me. I had changed, and there was no going back.

"So you're Talbot's tame fence," I said as I took the chair in front of the desk. Sammie lifted his arms halfway and dropped them.

"What can I say? Talbot made me an offer I couldn't refuse. I help them run a sting in return for complete immunity. I don't like doing it, but I've got my daughter to think of, too. If I go to jail, what happens to her?"

"Talbot really knows how to put the screws on, doesn't he?"

"Yeah. When I added it up, I really didn't have a choice." He shook his head. "And what about you, Kid? I thought you quit the business for good."

"So did I. Talbot got to me, too, and there were no good choices." I didn't volunteer any details, and Sammie didn't ask.

I dumped my collection of stolen goods on Sammie's desk. Sorting through the wallets and watches wasn't as much fun as it had been in the old days, knowing it was all going to be returned. Sammie took notes on each item as I matched the watches and wallets. The only watch without a wallet belonged to Tom Driscol. Sammie raised his eyebrows when I gave him the name. "I couldn't help it," I admitted.

He smiled a knowing smile.

"Well, that's it," he said at last, putting the list with the stuff and sweeping it all into a cloth bag. "I'll pass this on to Talbot's people, and they'll get it returned to the rightful owners in a week or so."

Our business concluded, I got up to leave. Sammie walked me over to the secret door and triggered it to open.

"Kid," he said, as I made to step through the door. Concern was written across Sammie's chubby face. "Watch out for Doris Whitaker. She's got all the pickpockets in town working for her now. She's not going to like you being back in business and not working for her."

"You're the second person to tell me that this morning. She really has all the dips under her control?"

"Yeah, and she's got enough muscle working for her that no one's going to cross her."

I thanked Sammie for the warning. Just what I needed as I went back to my life of crime. I tried to give him some assurance.

"I can handle Doris and her crew," I told Sammie and left.

I doubted Sammie believed it any more than I did.

Fifteen

"I've got bad news, Kid." Cochran and I were having coffee at a little shop down near the wharves. It was early Tuesday afternoon. Wolfe's courier was due to arrive the next morning.

"What is it this time?"

"Wolfe's courier isn't coming in tomorrow. He's not due until the day after."

Another day of working the street. I considered the ramifications.

"You know that Lynn really hates I'm picking pockets again, don't you?"

Cochran nodded. "I'm sorry, Kid. If I had known what a mess this would become, I would never have suggested your name to Talbot as the person to teach me how to pickpocket."

We drank our coffee in silence. Finally Cochran spoke up, and when he did it was with a subdued voice. "I'm not certain how much I should say to you, but I feel like I've got to tell you a few things about my boss, Mister Lawrence Talbot." He swallowed and continued. "I called Riley last night. There are some things about this operation that bother me and, well, he's kind of my mentor, you know."

I nodded but didn't reply, not wanting to interrupt his flow.

"Riley tells me that Talbot is straight, but," his voice trailed off.

"But?"

"But he's also very ambitious. In the Bureau you only have a few years to make a name for yourself, to get noticed by the higher-ups and tagged as someone who can work at the top levels. Talbot's running out of time on that, and Riley thinks he may be pushing this operation a little too hard in order to get a big win."

"I'd say it's more than a little."

"Yeah, it's starting to look that way to me, too. The problem is there's nothing you or I can do about it. So far everything he's done has been within the rules."

"Including threatening Barbara with arrest and taking The Book Nook from Lynn and me?"

Cochran motioned to me to keep my voice down. I did, but I was still pretty damned mad. "That guy comes in and forces me to go back on the street picking pockets. Lynn's furious, and Barbara's sick with worry. And you say that's within the rules?"

"Like it or not Kid, it is. Look, I said I was sorry, and I meant it."

I took a deep breath. I trusted Cochran and knew it wasn't his fault. "So, did Riley have any advice?"

"He suggested that we—you and I, that is—document everything so that if things blow up we don't get burned."

"We? How would you get burned? You work for Talbot."

"Talbot's got a reputation for pushing blame off onto those working for him." Cochran gave a tight smile. "After I talked with Riley I spent a fair bit of time going over the emails I've had from Talbot. I noticed something."

I raised an eyebrow.

"I noticed that he always words things so it looks like he's advising caution, and I'm the one pushing the envelope. That way, if things go wrong, he can cite them to put the blame on me."

"And if things go well?"

"He's the one who will write the report."

"History is written by the victor," I quoted.

"That's for certain."

"So where does that leave us?" I asked as I finished my coffee. Cochran drained the last of his, too, grimacing at the grounds at the bottom.

"Kid, that leaves you and me," then he added, "and Lynn and Barbara as pawns on a chessboard in a game where none of us have any say in what happens."

We took leave of each other after that. Cochran melted back into the shady world of the wharves while I made my way to a bus stop. I decided to work the plaza for another hour or two. As I rode back toward downtown and to Knickerbocker Lane, I had a vision of the city and the blocks I was traversing with each block a square on a chessboard and all of us simply pieces being moved by outside forces.

Sixteen

Any doubts I had about my return to a life of crime being believed were dispelled the next morning.

I had settled into a routine of lifting a few wallets late every morning, heading to Sammie's to get rid of them as quickly as possible, then heading home to The Book Nook and my real life of a respectable book store owner.

That morning started the same as the others. Lynn and I woke, showered and dressed. We did this with our usual efficiency and with little competition for the shower and bathroom. After a year of marriage it still surprised me how easily we had settled into living together. We joined Barbara for breakfast downstairs about nine. It was my turn to cook that morning, so I scrambled some eggs in an old iron skillet, snipped some green onions with my kitchen scissors, sliced a few mushrooms and made toast in the oven. I'd given up on ever finding a toaster that actually toasts.

Lynn, Barbara and I chatted about our plans for the day and the chores that needed doing. We traded ideas about dinner for the next few days with Barbara proposing a Mulligan stew for the next evening, the ingredients of which would depend on what she found at the farmers market that morning.

After breakfast I gave Lynn a kiss and headed out to pick some pockets, feeling like the husband from a 1950s sitcom going off to the office. As I left I wondered how I would look in a fedora.

By midmorning that day I had grabbed two wallets and a wristwatch from prosperous pedestrians. I was working Fremont Plaza in the heart of the financial district, named for that rogue

John C. Fremont and a favorite stalking ground of mine in the old days.

The sun had burned off all trace of morning fog and warmed the air. The sound of car and bus engines competed with raucous music from an impromptu band of street buskers. I recognized Molly, a street vendor setting up her cart of warm cinnamon buns, and in spite of my large breakfast, I went over to buy one.

Molly was in her mid-sixties, and her weathered face testified to years of working on the street. When I was a young teen, hustling hard to survive, Molly used to let me have one or two of her leftovers for free at the end of her day. There were nights when they'd been all that kept me from going to bed hungry.

Molly's face lit up when she saw me. "Kid! How are you doing? I haven't seen you in like forever!" She beamed a gap-toothed smile at me.

"Hello, Molly. How's business?" This was no idle question. Molly paid close attention to what she picked up from her customers' conversations, and if the stories were true, she had built a comfortable nest egg for herself by acting on that information.

Molly checked to see if anyone was within earshot before answering and pitched her voice low. "There's going to be a take-over attempt on Trinity Corporation next week. Get some shares before Friday, and you could do well."

I shook my head. "Too rich a game for my blood, Molly, but I will buy one of those buns." I reached into my pocket for some change.

Molly smiled. "On the house, Kid, for old time's sake." She looked over my shoulder, and her eyes narrowed. "Are you expecting company?"

I looked and caught sight of someone making a beeline for me. It was Chad. I hadn't particularly enjoyed our encounter at the book fair, and from the look on his face I wasn't going to enjoy this one either.

As I turned back to face Molly and her cart, I caught sight of two more young men, both dressed in that preppy look like Chad, closing in on me from both sides.

"Guess I'd better skip the bun, Molly, but thanks."

She frowned. "Trouble?"

"Nothing I can't handle," I answered with a bravado I didn't feel. "I'll come back soon for that bun." I left Molly and walked toward Chad. His companions altered their paths to match mine.

"Hey, Kid," Chad said, as the three arrived and bracketed me.

I took my time answering, studying and trying to take a measure of how much trouble they might cause. Chad stood with his fists on his hips. The guy on my right cracked his knuckles. The guy on my left snapped some chewing gum. All three were dressed in the style demanded by Doris Whitaker of those in her gang. Just what I didn't need, three young thugs looking for mischief. "What's up, Chad?"

"Mrs. Whitaker wants to talk with you."

"Yeah," said the one with the chewing gum. "She said we should invite you to have lunch with her." I looked up at the sun, then at Chad.

"That's very nice of Doris," I replied. Chad's face darkened at my presumptuous use of his boss's first name. "But it's a bit early for me. Maybe later today?"

The guy on my right cracked his knuckles again. "She told us you might take some persuading."

I admit it. I'm not a fighter. I like to think I keep in shape, but I have no experience in street fighting, nor do I want any. I gave an exaggerated shrug. "Fine, I'm persuaded. Where to?" The knuckle cracker looked disappointed.

Chad, obviously the leader, answered my question.

"Mrs. Whitaker," he emphasized her title for me, "is waiting for you at The Empire Room. We'll take you there."

Seventeen

The Empire Room was a relic, a holdover from a time when men wore ties even when casually dressed, women wore gloves to go grocery shopping, and no man or woman would be seen in public without a hat. A columnist once wrote that anything a person needed to know about how the city was being run could be learned in the taproom of The Empire, and a woman's social position could be made or broken by where the *maître d'* seated her in the dining room.

Those days are gone from our city, lost to decades of change, but the past lingered on inside The Empire Room in the rich décor, tall chandeliers, and the snootiness of the clientele.

I was glad I had opted for a suit coat and tie that day as we entered and so avoided the embarrassment of being offered ill-fitting loaners to wear before venturing farther.

Two of my escorts peeled off and disappeared into the Tap Room Bar, leaving Chad to do the honors of escorting me into the dining room. Once through the heavy double doors of the main dining room, the air tasted of leather and well-polished brass mixed with the scent of fine roasted coffee. The room was mostly empty of customers as it was long past breakfast and too early for lunch. A waitress laid out table settings while another ran a quiet carpet sweeper under the tables.

The waitresses at The Empire Room were also a throwback to the days of the gentlemen's clubs. They all wore the same uniform of fishnet stockings, shoes with stiletto heels, a very short black skirt and a starched white dress shirt, full sleeved and fully buttoned with a red bow tie at the neck. Even their hair was anachronistic, worn in a high, puffy bouffant.

Chad led me to a booth at the other end of the long dining room where cream-colored sheer curtains allowed only rarified light to illuminate the august furnishings. A woman, finely dressed and with expensively styled blue-tinted hair, sat in the center of a curved booth. She sipped from a thin china cup and held one delicate and manicured little finger out straight. She watched as we progressed across the room and set the cup down in its matching saucer as we arrived.

"Hello, Kid. It's nice to see you again."

"Hello, Doris," I replied. "Nice to see you doing so well." I surveyed the dining room. "Business must be good." Doris Whitaker motioned with her hand.

"Please, sit down. There's something I'd like to discuss with you."

I sat across the table from her. Chad sat close by on my right. I had seen the look in his eye when I addressed his boss by her first name. He either resented my violation of protocol, or perhaps he was jealous, not that I cared.

We studied each other for a minute. Like The Empire Room where she holds court each day, Doris Whitaker is a holdover from an earlier time. Her dress, her hairstyle, the string of pearls around her neck—all were like an illustration from *Life Magazine* in the late1950s. Thick pancake makeup masked the lines that age had etched in her face, but I knew her outward appearance covered a criminal cunning that kept her alive and in business.

Our mutual inspection over, Doris got straight to the point. "Kid, I hear you're back in business."

"You heard right."

"Yet only days ago you told Chad that you were done with working as a dip."

"Yes, well after I saw how poor the competition was these days, I decided it was time to show how it's really done."

Chad made a slight hissing noise. Doris waved him quiet. "The point of my questions, Kid, is to let you know that things have changed in the year since you quit the street."

"Have they?" I tried to look innocent.

"Yes, Kid, they have." Doris picked up a butter knife from a small plate near her. It was silver, like the other tableware, and beautifully polished. I watched Doris turn the knife in her hands, and the light from the chandeliers reflected on its small, blunt blade. I had no reason to fear it, but a shiver went down my spine nonetheless.

"You see, Kid," Doris continued as she played with the knife. "I've taken over the pickpocketing business in town. All the dips work for me now, and I take care of them." She tried to look maternal, but she wasn't any better at it than I was at looking innocent. "It's a rough world out on the street these days, Kid. You'll find you will appreciate working for me."

I acted like I was mulling it over. "That's an awfully nice offer, Doris, but I'm afraid I have to turn you down. I don't think I would make a good employee."

The butter knife struck the plate as Doris dropped it. A waitress laying out silverware at a nearby table turned at the sound and looked at us.

Doris' eyes shot daggers at me.

"I don't think you understood me, Kid. I wasn't making you an offer. I was telling you how it is. I run the pickpockets in this town, and if you want to work the street and stay healthy, you won't fight me on this."

I reached across the table and picked up the butter knife, then leaned back in my chair. I gazed at Doris as if considering what she said, but all the time I was flipping that stupid, dull knife around my fingers.

Both Doris and her young thug Chad couldn't help watching. I let the knife weave between my fingers, its blade catching the light again and again. I gave a little flip to my hand and the knife jumped to my other hand where I continued its dance between my fingers. At the right moment I slapped it onto the table and stood up, catching both Doris and Chad by surprise.

"Sorry, Doris," I said, "but the answer's still no."

Chad tried to get to his feet, but when he tried to push his chair back he found I had placed one foot firmly on the rung across its base and instead, he just rocked back and forth looking foolish. Anger clouded Doris' face.

"See you later," I said and walked away. I was worried Chad might give chase, but I heard Doris tell him to let me go. As I left the dining room, I gave one of the high-heeled waitresses a wave, and she smiled in return. Those shoes may be murder to wear, but I guess I they don't ruin a sense of humor.

Eighteen

Cochran called me around midnight that night to let me know that Wolfe's courier had arrived and had checked into his hotel. Tomorrow I'd take his wallet.

The night went slowly, and it was a relief when morning finally came.

I dressed and slipped out, avoiding the strained scene that breakfast with Lynn and Barbara would have been. I walked the six blocks from tiny and forgotten Knickerbocker Lane, with its brick and brownstone buildings, to Market Street, where The Meridian Hotel and its twelve stories of chrome and glass lobby presided over the bustle of the morning traffic.

I arrived fifteen minutes early and pushed through the revolving doors. The Meridian Hotel was familiar and fertile ground to me. At this time of the morning the large lobby was always busy with people in a hurry, their footsteps sounding and resounding on the marble floor. Great glass elevators whisked guests from floor to floor with pneumatic sighs. The robotic keys of a grand piano in the far corner tinkled a cheerful tune that competed with the drone of dozens of conversations.

A steady stream of men and women clad in business suits walked past me from the direction of the front desk, stuffing receipts and wallets back into their coat pockets and purses. As I had told Cochran, the easiest way to lift a wallet is to let the mark show you where it's kept.

I crossed the lobby to the gift shop, where I bought a newspaper. As I returned to the front of the hotel I spotted Talbot and Cochran camped out in a pair of easy chairs. After one more look around I went back outside and waited on the sidewalk.

The plan was pretty simple. In a few minutes Joey would pull up in the Town Car, having called Zager, the courier, to let him know he was almost there. Zager would leave his room, come down in an elevator and head for the revolving doors and outside. I would go into the lobby, bump into him, take his wallet, keep walking over to the interior door to the hotel garage and make my escape. Nice and simple.

I hate simple plans.

There was no reason for anyone to give me a second look as I stood on the sidewalk outside the hotel. To a casual observer I was simply another man in a business suit reading a newspaper, waiting to meet someone. The only ones who took notice of me were a couple of taxi drivers who slowed, checking to see if I needed a ride.

At nine o'clock a sleek, black car pulled up in front, and I recognized Joey behind the wheel. It was time.

I pushed through the revolving doors and entered the hotel. Just as planned, Zager was walking toward me. I held my newspaper up to my face and walked right into my target, too quickly for him to step out of the way.

Piece of cake and smooth as silk I thought to myself as I reached into his coat and let my fingers grasp his wallet. But as I did, I heard a sound from behind him. It was an insistent, metallic sound, like a stack of quarters being dropped an inch onto a tabletop. The sound repeated half a second later, and then again. A quizzical look came to Zager's face. Then his eyes rolled up, his knees sagged, and he fell against me.

A tall, thin, almost cadaverous man walked toward me. Though he looked to be in his fifties and was dressed conservatively, he had long, gray hair tied in a tight ponytail. He carried an overcoat over his right hand and forearm. In a second he had passed by.

I laid Zager on the marble floor. He was gasping for breath. I doubted he had long to live. I slipped his wallet into my own pocket and hoped no one noticed. The concierge arrived and knelt down on the other side of Zager. I got back up and began walking away toward the garage entrance. Out of the corner of my eye, I could see Talbot and Cochran heading toward where Zager lay. I quickened my pace and reached the door, pushed it open and went through. I held the door as it closed and watched the scene in the lobby through a narrow crack.

Zager was lying on his back on the marble floor where I had left him. The concierge stood next to him, looking around for help. Joey came in through the revolving doors. I watched him kneel next to Zager and bend his head down close to the dying man. A few seconds later he got back to his feet and hurried back outside. Even from within the garage, I could hear the screech of tires as he took off in the Town Car.

The concierge scanned the lobby, his gaze coming to focus on the garage door I had open by a few inches. It felt like he was looking straight at me even though I knew the light was too dim for him to see my face. For a moment I thought he was going to head my way, but then people began crowding around him, including Talbot and Cochran. I let the door close.

It was well past time for me to leave. I walked quickly through a dim concrete maze of curved driveways and parking places, heading for the entrance on the opposite side of the hotel. Footsteps and car tires reverberated through the concrete structure, causing me to check behind me as I made my way.

I paused when I reached the street. No one appeared interested in me. I left the garage, turned right and began walking. I didn't stop for six blocks. Along the way I heard the sirens of police cars and an ambulance screaming toward the hotel. In a few minutes the police would be casting a net and searching for someone, anyone, who might have something to do with the daytime shooting death of a man in the lobby of a high-class hotel.

Nineteen

By the time Talbot and Cochran showed up, I was on my second cup of coffee at Dino's Diner. They slid into the booth across from me with serious looks on their faces.

"I saw him," I told them before they could ask any questions.

"Who?" asked Talbot.

"The guy who killed Zager. He walked right by me. Tall guy, thin, with a gray ponytail."

"Yes," said Cochran. "We saw him from where we were sitting."

"Who was he? What's this do for your plans?" I asked Talbot.

"Nothing," he said. "We'll let the local police handle it. It doesn't concern us." He accepted a cup of coffee from the waitress and then waited until she was out of earshot, then held out his hand. "Now if you don't mind, the wallet?"

I handed it over. Talbot opened it and began looking for the data card. In seconds his search became frantic. Cochran and I watched as he emptied its contents and turned it inside out. No data card.

Talbot raised his eyes from the wallet and trained them on me. "Where's the data card, Kid?"

"I didn't take it," I answered. "That wallet is exactly as I found it."

Talbot slammed his fist onto the tabletop making our coffee cups jump. "Listen here, Kid. If you think you can pull a fast one on me, you'd better think again. Now hand over that data card." His mouth had twisted into a snarl, and there was a twitch in his left cheek.

Cochran put his hand on Talbot's arm. "The Kid says he didn't take the data card, and that makes sense. He has no reason to hold out on us."

"Of course he does," said Talbot, "the oldest reason in the world. He thinks he can cut a deal with Wolfe." His eyes fixed on mine. "I'm telling you for the last time. Give me that data card."

It was his eyes that gave him away. He was trying to intimidate me, but in those angry eyes I could also see fear. There was something about this operation that Talbot had kept from Cochran and me. I leaned back in the seat.

"What's the real story? What's got you in such a panic?"

Talbot's eyes shifted from mine to Cochran's and back. I could see that Cochran was wondering the same thing. Talbot got to his feet without saying another word and stalked out of the diner.

Cochran and I eyed each other. "Now what?" I asked him at length.

Cochran shook his head. "I don't know, Kid. Talbot had an awful lot riding on obtaining that data card. Without it, the case he's been building against Wolfe doesn't hold up."

"The data card that Talbot thinks I took."

"I'll keep trying to convince him that you don't have it." Cochran picked up the wallet and put the scattered contents back inside. "In the meantime I'll get rid of this and let the local police know you're working with us. Wouldn't want an all-points bulletin to go out for you."

"And I suppose I have to keep up the pretense of working the street?"

"For only a few more days, I'd say. Remember, for your own safety we need to convince Wolfe that this was only a random theft."

I stood up, fished in my pocket for a few dollars to cover the cost of the coffee and a tip and tossed them onto the table.

"I sure hope you and Talbot know what you're doing."

Twenty

A feeling of being home washed over me as I walked into The Book Nook. The bell over the door sounded, and Junior came over and wove his way between my legs. This was where I belonged, not out on the street living some fantasy of being a prince of thieves.

The beads in the doorway parted, and Lynn came through. I looked at her with new eyes and realized that whatever happened, my first priority was to ensure I didn't lose her. As she came close I reached out and took her in my arms. After a long moment, Lynn pulled back and studied my face.

"What is it, Kid? What happened?"

I told her.

"Oh, my God. How do you feel?"

"Pretty awful. I didn't know the guy, but he died in my arms. I keep thinking I should have stayed, but there wasn't anything I could do for him."

"What's Talbot going to do?"

Her face clouded when I described Talbot's belief that I had taken the data card in order to run my own game.

"I knew we couldn't trust him. What happens next?"

"I have to keep working the street for a few more days." I held up my right hand in a faux Boy Scout salute. "And when that's over I swear I'm never going to pick another pocket, ever!"

The last words of my solemn vow were overshadowed by a cry of anguish from the back room. I knew it couldn't be Junior, as he was still weaving between Lynn's and my legs. "Who or what was that?"

Lynn gave a half-hearted smile. "Guess who's back?"

The banshee wailed again. This time I was able to recognize April Quist's voice. "What am I supposed to do?" she cried. "I mean, do I call the home office and say, 'Gee I'm sorry, but I've lost the Max Carson you sent me. Sorry about that, can you send me another?'"

"Guess what? Max is missing." said Lynn.

"I really, really don't like Max Carson," I muttered as we pushed through the beaded curtain.

Barbara was seated at the table sorting through the morning mail. April was pacing about the kitchen, her high-heeled boots clacking on the linoleum floor. Her arms were crossed tightly across her chest, and on her face was painted all the righteous indignation a twenty-four-year-old woman with a Masters in Fine Arts can muster. She saw Lynn and raised her arms in a plea for support.

"Is it my fault Max went out to have a good time and hasn't come back? Is it?" She didn't wait for an answer but turned her fury on me. "What the hell am I doing playing nursemaid to an old goat like Max anyway? I'll have you know that I'm a writer, too. I've had stories published in some of the best literary magazines around. You ever hear of *The Grapevine Journal*? They were going to publish one of my stories. At least they said they were, then they folded."

Her pacing had brought her to the table, and she sat down, her anger escaping like air from a leaking tire. "What am I going to do?" she moaned and put her face down on her arms. At least she wasn't wailing anymore.

Barbara reached over and patted April's arm. "Now, now. I'm sure we can find this author of yours." She looked at me. "It seems Max Carson went out for a drink last night and hasn't been seen since."

April said something into her sleeve. Barbara interpreted for us. "He has a radio interview at four this afternoon and a television appearance this evening."

April said something else into her sleeve. It sounded like, "Idols are walking near us and won't stop," but when Barbara translated it became, "I don't want to go back to working at the coffee shop."

All of a sudden I was very tired of Max Carson, April Quist and the whole business. "Miss Quist," I said sternly. "Max's book signing at our store was last week. Our business with him is concluded."

"Greg!" Lynn's tone was both shocked and sharp. I couldn't remember the last time she had spoken to me like that. I felt my face flush. "April needs our help. If you don't feel like helping her, you can go watch the store. Maybe you can sell some more of Max's books and make some more money off him." She paused, and Barbara nodded her agreement. "In the meantime Barbara and I will do what we can to help April." All three women glared at me.

"I'm sorry," I stammered and realized there was nothing else for it but to do as I was told.

I could hear them talking as I fussed around the storefront, straightening things that didn't need straightening, moving a book from one display to another and then back again. I could hear their voices but not what they were saying. The mood of the conversation must have improved, as after a while I heard outbursts of giggles from Lynn and April along with Barbara's infectious laugh. I decided to see if my banishment was over.

It was, or at least I was allowed into the back room again. I don't know what they had been talking about, but all three went silent as I came in. April looked at me, then at Lynn, and the two of them burst into laughter again.

I ignored their childishness and went to pour myself some coffee. There wasn't any. I looked at the three of them at the table with their coffee cups. Lynn raised hers. "Sorry," she mouthed.

I came over and sat at the fourth place at the table. "So have you figured out what you're going to do to find Max?"

Lynn gave a smug smile. "Yes, we have. You are going to go pick him up."

"You know where he is?"

Lynn showed me her cell phone and explained. "Candy sent me a text message a little while ago. She's got Max down at The Pink Poodle."

The Pink Poodle was the strip bar where Lynn used to work. Candy, a former stripper like Lynn, still worked there, taking care of the dancers.

April leaned her head on one hand with her elbow on the table and stared at Lynn with wide eyes. "Wow, you really were a stripper? That must have been so amazing. What an experience."

Lynn frowned. "An experience is what it was, April. Believe me, it's nothing glamorous."

I felt the conversation slipping away. "Why don't the two of you go pick up Max? You don't need me along." The truth was that I was remembering the last time I had been there–over a year ago–and the undignified way I'd left.

Lynn shook her head. "Donnie wants you to come get him. He didn't say why."

"Can I really come along?" April asked. "I'd love to see what it's like there."

I was about to say no when Lynn answered for me.

"I suppose all three of us can go. It will be nice to see the girls and Angus, if he's there." Angus was the bouncer, a huge mountain of a Scotsman. He had provided the propulsion for my exit on my last visit, not that I held that against him.

Lynn and April disappeared upstairs. Lynn wanted to change her clothes, and April wanted a tour of the dance studio on the top floor after that.

Barbara and I picked up the coffee cups, spoons and plates. I washed and dried them while she put out a simple lunch for us before we left. She paused as she sliced some bread.

"It will be safe, Kid, won't it?"

I gave voice to what I had been thinking. "I think so, maybe because Lynn and Miss Quist will be along. Donnie's a hood, but he's not going to cause trouble with so many witnesses around. At least I don't think so."

"That's why Lynn said she was going, too?" Barbara had read my mind.

"Yes, safety in numbers and all that. Besides, Donnie always liked her."

The sound of footsteps on the stairs announced Lynn's and April's return.

Barbara took my hand and whispered to me just before they came in. "Well, you watch out nonetheless." She squeezed my hand and dropped it before I could answer.

Our lunch took longer than expected, partly due to April's peppering Lynn with questions about her former work at The Pink Poodle, how she started as a stripper and what it was like, but eventually we were ready to leave. We decided to take April's car, as on our return there would be four of us, including the oversize Max, and Lynn's little Geo Metro wouldn't do.

The three of us trooped out the front door of the store to the sound of the bell jangling, Barbara crying, "Godspeed!" and Junior the cat meowing his complaint at our leaving. Just before the door closed, Lynn dashed back inside and then joined us on the sidewalk. She held a copy of Max's book in her hand.

"A peace present for Donnie," she explained.

"Good idea," I said, marveling as I do at least twice a day at how much smarter Lynn is than I am.

We reached April's rented sedan and piled into it. I sat in the back so that Lynn could provide directions to The Pink Poodle. April buckled herself in and pressed the power button. The car's dashboard lit up with gauges and LCD screens but without the purr or vibration of an engine. There was only the slight hum of an electric motor that increased in pitch as we pulled away from the curb.

"I understand why your car wouldn't be big enough, Lynn, but doesn't Greg have a car of his own?" April asked as she took the first corner.

Personally, I didn't think it was necessary for Lynn to explain to April that I had only gotten my driver's license a few months before, but evidently she felt it was.

"He still can't handle the stick shift when he has to stop on a steep hill. You should see him trying to juggle the clutch, the gas and the emergency brake."

April laughed.

I refrained from taking part in the conversation.

Lynn can be so funny at times.

Twenty-One

The Pink Poodle is a second-rate strip club in a third-rate part of town. Not much had changed in the year that had passed since I was last there. The street was still full of potholes, and the adjacent sidewalks were still cracked and crumbling. The nail salon on the far side was still in operation, but the pet store next to that was closed and boarded over. A neon pink French poodle, dim in the afternoon sunlight, hung over the door to the club.

Lynn pulled into the gravel-covered parking lot next door. The few cars in the lot were parked near the club's back door. Although The Pink Poodle opened at eleven in the morning, the strippers didn't start their routines until three in the afternoon. Aside from a few habitual barflies, there wouldn't be many customers.

I watched April as we walked from the parking lot around to the front of the building. I could tell from her expression as she stepped around a puddle of oily water that so far, she wasn't too impressed.

We reached the front. The marquee windows were made of unbreakable acrylic that had turned yellow and brown with age. Pinup photographs of the dancers were tacked inside. April cast an inquisitive eye over them and then turned to Lynn.

She didn't have to ask, Lynn knew what the question would be.

"Yes," she said with a sigh. "I still have my photo." Lynn gave a theatrical shudder. "I'll show it to you later."

I opened the red door and held it for Lynn and April, then followed them inside.

The interior of The Pink Poodle is forever dim and shadowy, the better to mask the cheapness of the furnishings. Since the floorshows didn't begin for a while yet, it was relatively quiet with a recording of Sinatra crooning in the background. A sniff of the stale air brought back memories of when this was my hangout, back when Lynn worked here. It seemed like a lifetime ago.

The small dancer's stage with a pole in the center was across from where we stood. A pair of harsh, white lights gave it a flat and washed out appearance. Two young women dressed in jeans and sweatshirts were wiping the stage down with towels.

"Know them?" I asked Lynn.

She shook her head. "Newbies." She turned to April. "That's the first thing you learn when you're a stripper, how to keep the stage clean. Believe me, when you're dancing fast barefoot, you don't want anything on the floor, especially since there's no stopping the dance, ever."

The two young dancers had already wiped down the runway behind the bar. It ran the length of the side of the building to our left. Three men in rumpled coats had their elbows on the bar and their heads down in their drinks.

Even the Johnny the Bartender was the same as before. He gave me a glance to make certain I was watching and then turned his back on me. That didn't bother me. I felt the same way about him.

"Lynn! Kid!" Candy burst out from the door to the kitchen. "Thank God you're here." She hurried over and gave both Lynn and me a hug, then turned and examined April Quist. "You must be Miss Quist," she said and extended her hand. "Max was beginning to think you'd abandoned him."

April hesitated a moment before accepting Candy's welcome.

Candy was dressed in a heavy flannel bathrobe. Her hair was a tangle of an impossible shade of red with gray roots showing in places. She carried a few extra pounds, her makeup needed touching up and the slippers on her feet were decidedly un-sexy. For all that, Candy radiated beauty and a natural sensuousness.

"Hi, I'm April, Mister Carson's event coordinator. Is he okay?" It was interesting to watch the two women size each other up.

"Well, Donnie and his guys were pretty rough on him 'cause of all the damage he did." Candy pointed to a corner where several broken chairs were stacked. "They stuck him in a storeroom after he passed out."

Candy motioned to us to follow her as she continued. "I found him there this morning when I was getting a fresh can of coffee. He didn't wake up until a couple of hours ago."

We followed Candy back into the kitchen. This was a dreary room with windows made opaque with years of grease and wooden cabinets and counters that carried the scars of much use and little cleaning or care. The air had a rancid taste.

Max Carson, Famous Author, sat on a stool at a tall kitchen table, looking very different than when we had last seen him at the book signing at The Book Nook.

His hair was a matted mess. His long handlebar mustaches went in different directions, and the beginning of a black eye was showing above his right cheek. His clothes testified to his having spent hours sleeping on the floor.

"Oh, Max," cried April and hurried over to him.

Max gave a sheepish smile. "Hello, little lady. Did you come to bail me out?" He noticed Lynn and me. "Hey, you even brought the cavalry with you." Candy walked over and stood next to him as he continued. "April, Greg, Lynn, I'd like you to meet Miss Candy, my savior and protector."

Candy patted Max's hand. "Max, I told you that Lynn and The Kid are old friends of mine."

"Wait a second," Max rubbed his temple. "Are you sayin' the bookseller here is the guy who's going to square things for me? You told me it was some famous dude called The Kid."

"Max, that's how Greg is known around here. Don't worry, he'll talk with Donnie and straighten things out."

Max squinted his eyes and gave me an appraising onceover.

"Well, son, sounds like there's a bit more to you than I thought."

I waved that off. "What happened, Max?"

Max proceeded to tell a tale of personal heroism in the face of overwhelming odds. It had something to do with him rescuing a damsel in distress.

"Actually," Candy confided as she walked with me to Donnie's office, "Max was roaring drunk and for some reason decided that Kaitlyn was being mistreated by an important customer."

I didn't like the sound of that. "Just who was it?"

"Dom DeMarco."

"It would be. Max sure can pick them." Dom DeMarco wasn't part of a crime organization or anything. He didn't have to be, he was that powerful in our town. "I assume Kaitlyn wasn't being mistreated by DeMarco?"

"No." Candy searched for the right words. "Let's just say she was giving him a private performance in a quiet booth."

I didn't press for further explanation.

Candy continued. "Anyway, Max started a fight." She gave a smile. "He did pretty well."

"Didn't Angus stop him?"

"He was about to, but that was when Max passed out."

"Max didn't actually hit DeMarco, did he?"

"Unfortunately, I'm afraid he did. He got in a punch to Mister DeMarco's face before his guys could stop him."

That was bad news. Even if I could square things with Donnie, Max might as well leave town for a while. If Dom DeMarco took a dislike to Max, his book promotion appearances in the city would be beset by all kinds of problems, none of them traceable back to Mr. DeMarco, of course.

We arrived at the door to Donnie's office. Candy knocked and then opened it. She gave my arm a squeeze as I went inside and closed the door behind me.

"Hey, Kid, long time, no see." Donnie sat behind a metal desk painted to resemble wood. The décor of his office was from the School of Early Seventies Bad Taste. I doubt the green shag carpet had ever been cleaned. There was a chair in front of Donnie's desk.

I stood behind it with my hands on its back.

"Hi Donnie. Likewise."

If you asked me to rate the people I know on a scale of one to a hundred with a hundred being my least favorite, Donnie would be somewhere around two hundred fifty. He was like a toad, both physically and personally. He was short and squat with pale skin that hadn't seen the sun in years. He kept his cheaply dyed black hair combed over an ugly balding pate. Donnie was a bully and a coward, but he was also the owner of The Pink Poodle and a minor league mobster, and therefore not someone to cross lightly.

"I got a half-dozen good chairs that aren't any good anymore because of this friend of yours, Kid."

"He's not my friend, but I get your point." I didn't see any reason to argue with Donnie. "I'll see that he makes good."

"You'll make good if he doesn't?" While it was worded as a question, I knew it wasn't.

"I'll make good if he doesn't." I hoped it wouldn't come to that. Our bank account wasn't too flush.

"Well, then, that's settled." Donnie's lips pulled apart, and I realized he was smiling. That put me on my guard. Donnie is not the smiling type. "Now maybe you can do something for me."

"That depends." I knew this was going too smoothly.

He leaned forward. "Joey's gotten himself in some trouble."

I considered how much I could tell Donnie. "I understand there was a shooting this morning, and he was there."

"He was doing some bodyguard work, but the body he was guarding got killed. I don't want to see him get tagged by the cops for something he didn't do."

"I thought he wasn't working for you anymore."

"My wife was some kind of cousin to his mother. Joey's not too bright, and my wife is worried about him. I told her I'd do what I can." He narrowed his eyes at me. "You have some kind of pull downtown as I remember."

"Hardly," I protested. "In case you haven't heard, I'm back working the street."

"Tell you what. You help out Joey, and I'll talk with Dom DeMarco and see if I can convince him to lay off your writer friend."

I didn't want to, but I didn't have much choice. "All right, I'll do what I can. Where can I find him?"

"He's at his sister's house." Donnie gave me the address and then lifted himself out of his chair. "Come on, we'll tell your writer friend he can go."

Candy had been waiting outside Donnie's office and took my arm again as the three of us headed back to the kitchen, Donnie in the lead and Candy and I following.

Max, Lynn and April looked up as we came in. Candy put her hand on Max's shoulder. I went to stand beside Lynn and took her hand. She squeezed mine, and I gave a squeeze in return to let her know things were cool with Donnie.

Donnie frowned at Max and then pointed his finger at him. "You're a lucky guy. The Kid here is willing to vouch for you. I'll try to calm down Mr. DeMarco, but you'd better stay out of sight for a while."

"Stay out of sight?" asked Max. "I'm living in a hotel room and doing book signings every day."

"I've got an idea," said Candy. "He can stay at The Book Nook."

Max eyed her with admiration. "That's a great idea, little lady."

Candy beamed, and April frowned.

Lynn sighed. "I guess that would work."

My stomach sank. I turned to Donnie. "Just how long does Max have to keep out of sight?"

Donnie raised his hand and wiggled it. "A few days, maybe a week." He pointed a finger at Max. "I'll expect a check by the end of the week to cover those broken chairs. The Kid will tell you how much."

I could see that Max was about to argue about paying for the chairs, but Lynn stopped him. She held up the copy of Max's book. "Thank you, Donnie. By the way, Max would like you to have a copy of his book—signed, of course."

She put the book in front of Max and opened it.

Max hesitated.

April reached into her large purse and pulled out a pen. "Sign the book, Max," she ordered.

Max signed the book, closed it and handed it back to Lynn. She gave it to Donnie who felt the weight of it as though that was the way to judge a book.

"Huh, you wrote this? Thanks, I guess." I got the feeling that Donnie and books were not well acquainted. Donnie hefted the book again and then left.

Max got to his feet with Candy's help. "I guess it's been a long time since I slept on a storeroom floor," he explained. "I don't remember getting so stiff and sore in the old days."

The five of us left by way of the back door with Candy on one side of Max and April on the other. At the last minute Candy decided she should accompany Max back to the bookstore. We waited by the car while she ran in and quickly changed.

We had just enough room for all of us in April's sedan. April, of course, had the driver's seat, and Max took the front seat, as his long legs could never have fit in the back.

April turned on a built-in GPS and fed in the address of The Book Nook. Max made an effort at entertaining us on the trip back by trying to imitate the English-voiced device. He wasn't successful at either.

Lynn, Candy and I leaned back in the comfortable backseat and did our best to ignore the noise from up front.

"I could get used to this," said Candy, sitting on my right.

"Mmmmm," agreed Lynn from my left.
All in all, I had to agree.

Twenty-Two

Barbara greeted us as we trooped through the front door of The Book Nook. "Kid, Agent Cochran and that dreadful Agent Talbot are in the back room waiting for you."

Max overheard her. He put his hand on my arm as I started to head into the back. "Wait just a second there, son. I got some questions for you, starting with who and what the hell you are?"

"I run a bookstore, Max."

He crossed his arms and eyed me. "So what's with this Kid, stuff? And how is it that you've got pull with mobsters like that guy back at The Poodle? And why are there guys named Agent Cochran and Agent Talbot waiting to talk to you?"

I shook my head. "Not now, Max. Maybe later."

Lynn took my hand. "I'm coming, too, Kid. This involves both of us, you know."

As Lynn and I went into the back room I heard Max ask Barbara about Lynn and me, and I wondered what she would tell him.

Cochran and Talbot sat at the kitchen table in the back room. I noticed Barbara hadn't offered them coffee or tea. Talbot didn't waste any time.

"We still don't know who or why someone murdered Zager this morning, but the data chip is still missing, and Wolfe's got his men out hunting for it."

Lynn faced Talbot. If looks could kill, I wouldn't have given much for Talbot's life expectancy.

"Does that mean they'll be coming after Greg? He's the one who took the wallet, after all." She turned away for a moment, then swiveled back again, her eyes flashing with anger. "Or maybe they'll come after Barbara and me, or maybe burn the store down with us inside. Just a little more collateral damage, I suppose?"

"I understand your anger, Ms. Vargas, but we don't think any of you are in any danger. The word I've received from the man I have inside Wolfe's organization is that it's been totally accepted that your husband stole the wallet without knowing what was inside."

That didn't do much to quiet either Lynn's fears or mine.

"So that's it?" she demanded. "That's all you've got to offer?"

Cochran lifted his head and gave Lynn a sheepish smile.

"No, he's also offering me." It took a moment for his words to sink in.

"You're kidding," I said. "You're moving into The Book Nook again?" It was like a bad dream. "No offense, Cochran, but you have to admit that having you live here last time didn't do anything to stop someone from grabbing Lynn, torching the store and almost killing Barbara."

Talbot got to his feet. "Like I said, I don't believe you are in any danger." He gestured to Cochran. "But at Agent Cochran's request, I'm willing to let him stay here a few days until all this blows over." He took a step toward the door to the front of the store. "Now if you'll excuse me, I've got work to do." With that, he turned, and the curtain swished in his wake. A few seconds later we heard the bell over the shop door jangle as he left.

Lynn and I sank into chairs at the table. I looked at Cochran and shook my head. "Seems like old times, I guess."

He smiled. "I've got my stuff out in my car. I didn't think I should bring it in just in case you said no."

"You may as well go get it," I said and turned to Lynn. "Where do we put this one? If this keeps up, the city is going to hit us with a hotel tax."

"Who else is staying here?" Cochran asked.

I explained about Max Carson's predicament and why he was taking up space for a few days at The Book Nook. After a few moments the same thought came to all three of us.

Lynn said it first. "We're going to have to tell Max about what's going on. If he's here, that means he could be in danger, too."

"Possible danger," Cochran corrected. "The truth is that everything we know suggests otherwise."

"Still, Lynn's right," I said. "We may as well get it over with. Let's go and introduce everyone, and then we can figure out who's sleeping where and what the shower schedule will be in the morning."

Twenty-Three

Max Carson slapped me on the back as we trooped out of the back room and into the store. "Well, I'll be!" He looked me up and down like a ten-year-old boy meeting a stage magician. "A pickpocket, eh? If that don't beat all."

"A master pickpocket," Candy corrected.

"A former pickpocket," I corrected in turn. "I gave all of that up a year ago."

"That's not what people are saying at The Pink Poodle and out on the street, Kid," returned Candy. "Seems every day someone comes up to me to tell me that you've gone back to working the street." She stopped talking when she realized Cochran was with us. "Don't I know you?"

He stepped forward and offered his hand. "Yes, I met you last year at Lynn and Greg's wedding."

"Oh, right. You're one of those FBI agents, aren't you?"

"That's right. I'm Agent Cochran."

Max slapped his leg. "Okay, now stop right there." He turned to Candy. "You told me that Greg here is a notorious pickpocket. I get that. But what's a federal agent doing in all of this?"

The next fifteen minutes were spent explaining in vague terms why it was that I was pretending to have gone back to a life of crime, as well as why Max's staying with us could put him in another kind of danger.

"Hell, Kid. You don't mind if I call you Kid, do you? I think it kind of fits you better than Greg. Besides, that's what Sweet Candy calls you."

Candy beamed, April frowned, and this time it was my turn to shrug.

Max continued. "I'm already in trouble with that DeMarco guy. If I'm going to lay low, I may as well do it where there's a federal agent standing guard." He cocked an eye at Cochran. "Though I can't say you look much like a fed, no offense."

"None taken," said Cochran. "I've been working undercover the past few months, so I guess it worked."

Candy glanced at the clock. "Oh, I've got to get back to the club." She turned to Lynn. "Do you think you could give me a ride back? I can take a bus if it's any trouble."

"I can give you a ride," April offered. "I have to head back to the hotel and pick up some things for Max and me, and I can swing by there on the way back." They were gone out the door before her words sank in.

"Did I hear her say she's picking up her things, too?" I asked Lynn.

She nodded. "Looks like we're going to have a full house."

Barbara took my arm. She had a big smile on her face.

"Oh, Kid. It's just like the old days."

Twenty-Four

That night was like the first night of camp, not that I'd been to one, but it certainly fit the popular idea of it. We all stayed up far too late, drinking Belgium beer and pots of tea. I had to bring up some extra chairs from the basement so that we could all sit in the kitchen.

We spent most of our time swapping stories. Barbara reminisced about the days of the anti-war movement and the people who had stayed at The Book Nook. Her eyes grew misty as she remembered not only friends from more than forty years before, but the passion and commitment they had to their cause. April asked Lynn dozens of questions about her days as a stripper, much to the amusement of Max.

"Now young lady," he said, in the manner of a stern, elder uncle, "what would your parents say if you threw away that master's degree and took up dancing in a place like The Pink Poodle?

April blushed and didn't answer.

Cochran loosened up enough to tell us a few stories of stakeouts and arrests, and Lynn told a few tales about life at The Pink Poodle. I told the story, legendary among pickpockets, of how my mentor, Fast Eddie Dupree, had removed a necktie from the chief of police during a press conference without anyone noticing.

But it was Max who told the best stories that night. I had to admit once again that for all the annoyance Max had caused, he was one heck of a storyteller. The night grew later and later as he spun one tale after another about how he began as a writer. No MFA program for Max. His alma mater was the street, and his first paying job as a writer was as a reporter for a well-known scandal sheet.

"Reporter? Hell, we weren't reporters. Most of the stuff we wrote about we made up. The editor required us to come up with a dozen stories a week about celebrities misbehaving, flying saucers, grisly crimes, you name it." He took a long pull from his beer and wiped his mouth on the back of his hand. He thought for a second and then slapped his knee. "Do you know, we used to flip coins to see who had to put on the rubber suit while the rest of us took pictures of the spaceman walking around Central Park?"

When the laughter around the table subsided, I asked Max how he'd become the author of best-selling books, given his start.

"I'm no author, Kid," he corrected me. "I'm a writer. There's a difference."

"What do you mean?" asked April.

I got the feeling she was seeing a new side of Max and the publishing business, one very different than she had learned while earning her master's degree.

Max took another swig of beer from his bottle and thought before he answered.

"Well, young lady, it's like this." He waved his hand at the beaded curtain that led to the store. "Out there you've got what? Three, four thousand books?"

I closed my eyes and did a quick tally. "About forty-five hundred, all but fifteen hundred of them used."

Max nodded. "Okay, and some of those books are by people like Gaiman, Chabon, and that Kenyon lady, bless her heart. To my mind, those are authors. They work very hard at writing what people call literature. Sometimes it takes one of those authors a decade or more to turn out a book, and make no mistake, those are damn well-written books." He paused and stroked his mustache, then pointed at his chest. "Then there are writers like me. We crank out a book every year, sometimes faster. I won't claim my writing holds a candle to those others, but you know what? People like to read them."

"And you make a lot of money," said Lynn.

Max slowly shook his head. "Sorry, little lady, but for a mid-list author like me, the money's not all that great. The publishers only pay for part of the expenses of these tours." He nodded at April. "I'm lucky my publisher lent me Miss April while I'm in town." He shook his head again and then smiled widely. "But hey! I get to hang out with you guys in the back of a bookstore and drink beer and tell stories. Life's not so bad, is it?" He let out a roar of laughter.

Such was his infectious spirit that we all laughed with him without really having cause to do so, or perhaps because of that.

Twenty-Five

The next morning I became aware of someone following me soon after I left The Book Nook. I can't claim to be an expert at spotting a tail, but in this case it wasn't too hard. I waited for him to catch up with me at the street corner. It was Max Carson.

I crossed my arms. "Max, what are you doing? You can't follow me."

His face had a sheepish look. "I was sort of hoping to tag along and watch you pick some pockets." He held up a palm, "Hey, you never know, I may be able to use it in a book."

I was going to say no, but then he added, "I'll buy you lunch?"

I gave in. "Oh, the heck with it," I said. "Come along. I've never had an audience before, but," I gave him a sideways look, "as long as I get to pick the place."

"So long as it doesn't involve vintage bottles of wine or food I can't pronounce, no problem. Where?"

"Dee's Italian Beef," I told him. "It's the best sandwich in the city."

That sealed the deal for Max.

We crossed the street and turned the corner on Oak. As we walked I tried to give Max a series of conditions to his watching me at work. Foremost of these was, "Stay a good way's away, and don't look at me directly. I really don't need to be caught at this point."

As we walked toward City Square, I noticed I had to slow my pace for Max and realized he had a slight limp. He caught me looking and explained with another of his stories. This time it was when he was fifteen and fell off the roof of a building under construction at night with his friends, and after consuming a significant quantity of alcohol.

"Oh, man," said Max, shaking his head, "To this day, I don't know how I managed to survive that fall. I had no idea how hurt I was at first. Then I noticed the bottom of my foot was facing me at an angle that couldn't be good. It turned out my leg was broken in three places."

He gave me one of his over-powered slaps on the back. "But who cares about that stuff, right, Kid?"

I began to answer and then realized Max was no longer walking next to me. He had veered over to a store window and was standing in front of it, staring at a poster.

We were in front of the bookstore at City Center, and of course it was one of his own posters at which Max was staring. The photo showed him in the classic author pose, turned at an angle from the camera, looking back with an intense and knowing stare.

Max turned and saw that I was watching. He backed up against the window, next to the poster, and then struck the same pose but with an exaggerated, almost bug-eyed stare.

I couldn't help laughing, and he joined in as he walked back to me.

"Isn't that the stupidest goddamned thing you ever saw?" he asked me. "I spent three hours in that photographer's studio. He took picture after picture, one pose after another." He grinned. "Apparently my good side isn't easy to find."

I noticed a sidewalk vendor I knew across the street. "Wait here," I told Max and cut across the stopped traffic.

Carl is a third-generation street vendor of walking sticks and canes. There's a sense of timelessness to Carl and his cart. You could pick up both his cart and him and drop them down on a city street of a hundred years ago, and they would fit right in.

"Hi, Kid," called Carl as I approached. "How's tricks? I hear you're back on the street."

I gave Carl a vague answer and rooted through his collection of canes. It didn't take me long to find what I was looking for. It was a gentleman's walking stick made of black ebony and topped by a heavy silver head of simple design. Carl raised his eyebrows.

"It's for a friend of mine."

"Sure, Kid. No problem." Carl named his price. I countered, and we settled somewhere in between. I was going to have to explain the expense to Lynn, but I figured she wouldn't mind.

I had made certain to stand in a way so that Max couldn't see from across the street what I was buying. I took the walking stick and pushed the small end up my sleeve as far as it could go, without it poking up and distorting the shoulder of my jacket. This left a good deal of it extending down from my hand, but by holding said hand against my leg, I was able to keep it from view as I walked back to where Max was waiting.

This time I took the crosswalk and made certain I had to wait for the signal to change. Max's curiosity was written on his face by the time I got back.

"Hey, Max," I said. "I've got a present for you. Hold out your hand." He did that and I extended my hand and placed the head of the walking stick in his. He took hold, I stepped back, and the rest of the cane came into view.

Max's smile reached all the way to his eyes. He held up the walking stick and admired it both its looks and its heft. "Well, thank you, Kid. Such a handsome thing." He tapped the stick on the pavement. "I accept."

We continued back on our way with Max swirling the walking stick in a dandy, debonair fashion.

Soon we reached City Square and split up, though not before I reminded Max of the rules.

The fall weather, the overall good nature of the people out and about that day, all converged to create an ideal place for me and other pickpockets. Jackets and coats were worn unzipped and undone. People were distracted by the sounds of street musicians, the hum of a hundred conversations, the cell phones in their hands.

Knowing that Max was watching, I took my time choosing my first mark. Several minutes later I spotted a likely target, yet another businessman walking toward me, cell phone to his ear.

I changed my direction and picked up my pace, angling to intersect with him in about twenty paces. His left front pocket would be my first dip. If there was nothing there I'd have, I hoped, time to check the right side of his coat. If his wallet wasn't in either place, then I'd have to move on and find another mark.

At five paces out a loud shout came from behind me.

"Stop him! Stop that kid!"

My target and pretty much everyone else stopped walking to watch what was going on behind me. I had no choice but to do the same.

A teenager in jeans and a hooded sweatshirt ran across the square, chased by a middle-aged man in a suit.

"Stop him," the man called. "He stole my wallet."

The boy ducked and dodged through the pedestrians and might have made it had not someone stuck out a leg and tripped him. He went flying and landed flat on his stomach. It looked like his breath had been knocked out of him as he lay there, gasping for breath.

His victim hurried up to him, reached down and grabbed a wallet from the kid's hand. A uniformed policewoman walked up as the man was checking its contents.

I was too far away to hear what was said, but it wasn't necessary to hear the words to know what was happening. The policewoman put handcuffs on the boy and helped him to his feet. His nose was bleeding. My sympathies were with the boy, I have to admit. That would have been me not too many years ago, with my hands in cuffs and blood on my face.

I sensed someone walking near me and heard the tapping of a cane on the pavement. I didn't have to look to see who it was.

"Maybe we should try another time," Max said, considerately.

I nodded. He was right. Everyone would be on their guard for a while.

Max's cell phone rang. He answered it, spoke briefly and then put it away.

"That was Miss April," he said. "She and Candy are swinging by to pick me up. It seems I've got another appearance to make."

We walked over to the Market Street side of the plaza, and only a minute later April's car pulled over. Candy was in the passenger seat.

Max clapped me on the shoulder. "Another day, eh, partner?" He opened the rear door and climbed in. The door shut with a thud. Candy waved to me as they pulled out into traffic.

Only after they disappeared from view did I realize that Max never did buy me that lunch.

Twenty-Six

The next morning I took a break from boosting wallets. I had promised Donnie I'd try to help Joey. Donnie's idea was that I'd use my supposed pull with the FBI to keep Joey out of jail. My idea was that Joey might know where that damned data card was. Lynn's idea was that she would go along. I knew better than to argue.

We headed out in her little Geo Metro to visit Joey's sister. Candy had sent word the evening before that Esther might know where he was hiding. We puttered through the late rush hour traffic downtown and down Prospect Avenue to the outer districts.

The neighborhood of Butchertown got its name back at the turn of the previous century when the nascent city's meat packing businesses were congregated over the hill from the rest of the population, where a strong bay breeze kept the smell of the slaughterhouses from spreading inland.

A hundred years later the meat packinghouses and their smells were gone, but remaining were blocks of small craftsman houses and cottages. The neighborhood has yet to fall prey to gentrification, so these remnants look much as they did in decades past with paint peeling, roofs in need of repair and front yards growing more weeds than grass.

We drove along potholed streets until we found the address we wanted. Lynn parked across the street, and we got out and studied the house where Joey's sister lived. It was much like its neighbors, narrow and long, and it extended most of the way to the back of its lot. Inside, I imagined it was a typical shotgun layout with the livingroom in the front, then a hallway down the side of the house all the way back to the kitchen with occasional doors opening on bedrooms and one bathroom.

We went across the street and up the old concrete walkway to the front door. I knocked on the screen, rattling it as best I could, as there was no doorbell visible. There was no response. I knocked again, louder. This time a voice came from somewhere within the house, telling us to wait a minute.

The minute passed, and its passing brought the sound of someone walking toward the door. A few seconds later a figure appeared behind the screen.

"Who are you, and what do you want?" a woman's voice demanded.

"Esther?" I asked.

"Who wants to know?"

I gave my name and told her I was looking for Joey.

"Joey ain't here. Now go away." She turned and walked away.

"Let me try," Lynn said.

She rattled the door again. "Joey," she called. "It's Lynn. Lynn Vargas. You remember me from The Pink Poodle? I was one of the dancers. I'm here with The Kid. We need to talk."

There was another long silence, and then we saw the woman's figure shuffling toward us again. She unhooked the screen door and opened it. She looked at us with suspicion and then cast an eye up and down the street. Appearing satisfied, she motioned us inside and latched the door behind us. We followed her down a long, dimly lit hallway with walls covered in wallpaper that probably was original to the house. She stopped in front of a closed door and rapped with her knuckles.

"Joey, they're here. They look okay." We heard the sound of a key turning in a lock, and then the door opened. We slipped inside, and the door shut behind us. I heard the lock click again. Lynn and I turned and faced Joey.

He was the same and yet different. The Joey I knew from The Pink Poodle days provided muscle for Donnie. Big and beefy, he had a confidence in his size and menace that flowed from him like the cheap cologne he wore.

Joey moved a few feet in the dim light and sat on the edge of an unmade bed. I studied the room. This must have been Joey's bedroom all through high school. There were posters of rock bands on the wall, a couple of small bookcases that mainly held wrestling trophies, and other odds and ends. Near the window, where the curtains were drawn tightly against the daylight, there was a small desk and chair, the kind called a student desk, made of cheap pressboard. I pulled the chair out and turned it to face the bed and offered it to Lynn. She sat while I leaned against the desk, being careful not to put too much weight on it.

Poor Joey. He looked miserable and seemed to have shrunk to only half his size. His hair, normally slicked back and combed, was a tousled mess, and his clothes were wrinkled and creased as though he'd slept in them, if he had slept at all. His face was puffy and unshaven.

"I'm in trouble, ain't I, Kid?"

"I don't know, Joey. What happened the other day? Why did you run?"

"He told me to."

"He? Who told you to run, Joey?"

"Mr. Zager. When I leaned over him after he got shot. He told me, 'Get out of here, Joey, or they'll get you, too.' So I did like he said. I got out of there."

I marveled at the ability of some people to do blindly as they were told no matter what was going on. A dying man told him to leave, so he did. Simple.

"Did you see who shot Zager?"

"Just a guy in a suit. Oh, yeah, he had a ponytail." Curiosity finally made an appearance in Joey's mind. "What's this all about, Kid?"

"That's what I'm trying to figure out."

"Well, I'll tell you another thing that's strange."

"Another thing?"

"Yeah. Mr. Zager was acting weird ever since I met him at the airport the night before. Usually he's cracking jokes and stuff, asking me about how I'm doing, that kind of thing. This trip he wasn't like that at all. Kept quiet all the way from the airport."

"You didn't stay with him at the hotel?"

"No. I always offered to, but he didn't think it was necessary. I came home and then went back the next morning to pick him up. Nine o'clock sharp. Those were his orders, and I was there on time." He shook his head. "I done this three, four times before. Never any trouble, and I never saw this coming. But maybe he did."

"How so?"

Joey was wary. "I don't know how much I ought to be telling you about this, Kid. I think I'm in enough trouble as it is."

Lynn got up from the desk chair and sat on the bed next to Joey. "We don't want you to get into trouble, Joey. It's just that everyone is looking for something that was in Mr. Zager's wallet, a data card. Do you know where it is?"

"You mean like they use in a computer or a camera?"

My hopes shot up and then dropped back down again.

Joey shook his head. "No, nothin' like that. I did just what I was hired to do. I picked up Mr. Zager at the airport and dropped him off at his hotel, just like I was told to do. I came back in the morning, just like I was told to do. It was no different than the other times I picked him up and dropped him off," Joey shrugged, "except for the part about him getting shot and all."

I tried again. "What did you mean when you said that maybe Zager expected trouble?"

Joey thought for a second. "Well, it sounds funny, but Mister Zager seemed to know something was going to happen to him. He told me he had a," Joey faltered as he searched for a word, "you know, one of those things where you know what's going to happen?"

"A premonition?" prompted Lynn.

"Yeah, that's it. He said he had a premonition," Joey sounded the word out carefully, "that someone was going to try something. I think that's why he was acting so strange, on account of that premonition." Again he sounded the word out syllable by syllable.

He checked an alarm clock on the desk next to where I was perched. "I got to go soon. He wants to talk to me."

"Who wants to talk with you, Joey?" asked Lynn.

"The guy who hired me," Joey answered.

"Who is that?"

Joey lifted his big shoulders and dropped them. "I don't know. I never met him. Hell, I never even talked to him. Mr. DeMarco told me when and where I was supposed to go."

Getting information from Joey was like nailing jelly to a tree, not that I've ever tried that. "Did Mr. DeMarco tell you that the man who hired you wants to meet you?"

Joey frowned. "No, he didn't." He pointed to the desk. "The guy called my sister on the telephone, and she wrote down the message for me."

There was scrap of lined paper on the desk. The writing on it was blocky and uneven. I picked it up and read it aloud.

"Tell Joey to go to the corner of 12th and Grant at eleven this morning. A car will pick him up."

Joey reached for the message, and I handed it to him. He folded it carefully and put it in his pants pocket. "See, Kid. I got to do what he says. It's the only way to show him I didn't have anything to do with Mr. Zager getting shot."

It was clear that Joey had made up his mind, and nothing we could say would change it.

"Can we give you a ride?" asked Lynn as we left the bedroom and walked down the dingy hallway toward the front door.

Joey thought about it. "I guess that wouldn't hurt," he admitted, "but you got to promise not to stick around or anything. I don't want to get into any more trouble."

We both promised, while avoiding looking at each other. I didn't want to get Joey into trouble but was hoping there would be a way to place ourselves where we could watch without him or anyone else noticing.

I had to squeeze into the back seat of Lynn's little Metro, sitting sidewise with my feet up on the seat next to me since Joey could barely fit into the front passenger seat even with it shoved all the way back. We rode that way to downtown with me, once again, feeling every pothole in the city.

My plans for spying on Joey were ruined when he displayed a little more cunning than I would have given him credit for.

"Pull over here," he said before we were at his pickup place. Lynn swerved over to the curb. Joey got out, and I removed myself from the back. "I'll walk from here. Thanks a lot for the ride."

Joey walked quickly to the corner and turned right. I got back into the car.

"Come on," I said to Lynn, "Let's follow."

She pointed to the one-way sign for the cross street. It pointed left. "No can do, Kid. By the time we go up another block and then work our way around to where he's being met he'll be gone."

I argued that we had time, and she humored me by giving it a try, but she was right, as she usually is. A long black car pulled from the corner where Joey was supposed to be but wasn't. It headed down a side street ahead of us, with no way for Lynn to make the turn in time to follow.

Stuck in traffic at the light, I watched the car as it drove away, wondering if Joey was inside and what was going to happen now.

Twenty-Seven

The next morning I got an early start to my renewed life of crime. I stumbled into the shower, then dressed and went downstairs long before Lynn was ready to get up.

Junior was crunching dry cat food in his dish in the corner, and Cochran was sitting at the kitchen table. He was already dressed, with a cup of coffee in front of him. He looked like he was waiting for me.

He was.

I wondered if he had learned about our visit the day before to see Joey. Lynn and I had decided to keep that to ourselves, at least for the time being. It turned out he hadn't, not that that made my conscience feel any better.

"Kid, you got a minute before you leave?" I poured myself a cup of coffee and sat down. Sun streamed in through the back window curtains. Junior finished his breakfast and walked over to my chair. I moved my leg, and he hopped up into my lap and began washing himself.

"What's up, Cochran?" I asked without preamble.

"I talked to Talbot a few minutes ago, and he told me something I think you should know." Cochran lowered his voice. "The thing is, you can't let on you know it. Talbot would have my hide if he found out."

I put the coffee cup down. "What is it?"

"Dennis Metcalf, Wolfe's lawyer and number two man, flew into town from the Caribbean last night."

"Are you going to pick him up?"

"That's what I asked Talbot. He said no, but he didn't say why. My guess is he doesn't want to alert Wolfe that we knew he was coming."

"And expose the mole Talbot has inside Wolfe's organization."

Cochran nodded.

"Okay," I said. "What does this have to do with me?"

"I'm worried, Kid. Metcalf is probably here to look into Zager's death and," Cochran paused and looked straight at me, "it's possible he's going to take a fresh look at you."

"What can I do?"

"Just keep on as before, but keep your eyes and ears open. If I'm right, there's going to be people asking about you the next couple of days."

With that disquieting news on my mind, I took my leave of the store. It was still early enough that the streets and sidewalks were full of people hurrying to work, and it was garbage pickup day on our block, but I paid little attention to the people or the smell as I mulled over what Cochran had told me.

I took a bus to the corner of Jackson and Nineteenth, across from the county courthouse, and resumed my charade of working the street.

It was a morning of easy pickings. Lawyers and their clients streamed by on the sidewalks, eager to make court dates. I targeted the lawyers, their roles made obvious by the formal clothes they wore in an age when casual Friday has spread to every weekday. I figured their clients had trouble enough without my adding to it.

I kept it up until noon, all the while wondering if I was being watched. I didn't spot anyone, and none of my marks twigged to what I was up to when I performed the dips. The fact was, and I would never admit this to Lynn and could barely admit it to myself, I found I was just as good picking pockets as I used to be.

Halfway through the morning I ran into Jay, the sidewalk fence, again. We exchanged pleasantries, all the time watching around us for potential marks and trouble. After a minute he cleared his throat.

"Kid, a guy came around asking about you."

I cocked an eyebrow at him. "A guy?"

"Yeah, you know, the kind of guy you don't want to mess with."

I knew just what he meant.

"What did he want?"

"It's kind of strange. He wanted to know if you were a pickpocket. I told him sure you are, one of the best. That's okay, isn't it?"

"Yes, it is," I assured him. Jay still looked troubled.

"I'm not a tough guy, Kid. I don't get involved in that kind of stuff. I mean, when someone like that comes along, I'm going to tell them what they want."

"That's okay, Jay. I know exactly what that's like. I'm no tough guy either."

"Well, okay, as long as you're cool with it." Jay shook my hand and left in his sideways sort of way.

What Jay told me gave me a lot to ponder, and I decided to quit for the morning and head over to Sammie's. It was an even cinch that the guy checking up on me with Jay was working for Wolfe. If I'd had any doubts about the necessity of keeping up the appearance of a working pickpocket, they were gone now.

I left Sammie's as the time was approaching noon. It was about three blocks from Sammie's shop to the M bus line, and I set out at a fast pace, eager to get back to The Book Nook and my real life.

"Hey, Kid! Wait!" A voice commanded from behind me. I turned around and saw Chad and another of Doris Whitaker's crew walking toward me. They must have been waiting outside

Sammie's for me. That didn't look good. I made a pretense of looking up at the sun.

"Gee, sorry guys. I'd love to stay and chat, but I'm due downtown in a few minutes. Why don't you call my office and make an appointment?"

The looks on their faces as they caught up to me showed that they didn't appreciate my sense of humor. Chad cracked his knuckles. The other one tried to do the same but without any sound.

Chad glared at him. "Cool it, Jeremy." He turned back to me. "Mrs. Whitaker has a message for you, Kid."

"Yeah, well, give Doris my best, but I don't have time."

I turned to leave. Chad grabbed my right arm and pulled me back around. Jeremy slugged me in the stomach and I doubled over, the breath knocked out of me.

Chad and Jeremy waited until I got a good lungful of air again and stood straight, or as straight as I could. My eyes watered. "Was that the message, or is there more?"

He gave a wolfish grin. "Mrs. Whitaker says you need to make up your mind. Are you going to work for her, or do we get to break all of your fingers?"

Jeremy chimed in. "One at a time, slowly." He pantomimed bending his own fingers back.

I did a quick calculation in my head. Talbot wanted me to keep working the street for another week, then I'd be off the hook. I held up my hands in surrender.

"Okay, you win."

Chad and his buddy looked disappointed.

"Ask Doris ..." I began. Chad raised a fist. "Ask Mrs. Whitaker if I can meet her for lunch at The Empire Room the day after tomorrow. She and I can work out the details then."

This confused them.

"What do you mean, work out the details?" Chad asked. "What's there to work out, smart guy? You work for Mrs. Whitaker, or we break your fingers."

"Are you kidding?" I waved my arm, the one closest to the street, widely. "There are covenants to be agreed on, equitable splitting of the proceeds, all kinds of details. Jeez, don't you remember what Mrs. Whitaker told you?"

My two erstwhile partners in conversation strained their memories, trying to figure out what I was talking about. Meanwhile I watched the gypsy cab driving toward us from behind them. As I had hoped, the driver had interpreted my arm waving as a customer flagging him down.

I pivoted on my heels as soon as the cab slowed to a stop, and in a couple of seconds had the door open, jumped in and shouted to the driver. "Go! Go!" He went.

Chad and Jeremy pounded on the side of the cab as we pulled away. I didn't bother looking behind.

"Where to?" asked the cabby, his eyes studying me in the rear view mirror.

"Just a few blocks," I answered. "Drop me somewhere along the M line." It wasn't that I wouldn't welcome a cab ride back to The Book Nook, but I didn't have that much cash on me. I shook my head. I had just left close to a thousand dollars in cash back at Sammie's to be returned along with the owners' wallets, and I didn't have enough of my own cash to afford a cab ride. This honesty business sure didn't pay well.

Twenty-Eight

Cochran was in the back room of The Book Nook when I returned. I told him about Jay's report that someone was asking about me. "That's good," said Cochran. He was sitting at the table, tapping on a laptop.

Lynn must have overheard us as she came down from her studio. "Good?" she asked.

"Yes. We want Wolfe and his people to be convinced The Kid is only a pickpocket. If they were to suspect otherwise," his voice trailed off.

"We get the picture," I answered. I gave Lynn a kiss. "So what's new back here at Hotel Book Nook?" I looked around the kitchen, but we were the only three in the room. "Old Tom is watching the store. Where are Barbara, Max and April?"

"Max, April and Candy are off at a radio station for yet another interview," Lynn told me. She poked my stomach, and I recoiled. She nodded. I have no idea how she figured it out that I had been slugged, but she did. Her next question told me that.

"How was the street this morning? Any problems?" Lynn looked me in the eyes as she asked that, and there was no way I could evade telling her.

"Well, a couple of Doris Whitaker's crew came after me. They made it clear," I touched my stomach, "painfully clear that I am expected to go to work for Doris.

Lynn frowned. "Or?"

"Or I get my fingers broken."

Lynn sucked in her breath. She turned to Cochran, "Can't you do something about this? It's one thing for The Kid to help your boss out, but what are we supposed to do now?"

Cochran motioned to the other chairs at the table. "Sit down and tell me about this Doris Whitaker."

We did, taking turns. In a few minutes Cochran knew as much as anyone who works the streets knew about Mrs. Whitaker, the Grand Doyenne of petty crime in our city. He found out about Doris's rise from a street huggermugger and roller of drunks to the faux society matron she plays today.

When we were through Cochran pointed to his laptop. "Give me a few minutes. I want to see what our database has on her." He turned to his laptop and began pecking at the keyboard.

Lynn and I went out into the bookstore. Old Tom waved from his perch behind the counter. Junior came strutting over and wove his sinuous form between our legs.

"So everyone's accounted for except Barbara," I said. "What is she up to?"

Just as I asked that question, the front door opened, and Barbara came in. Her face looked worn, but she smiled when she saw us. "Hello, Kid. Hello, Lynn." She gave us each a kiss on the cheek and then waved at Tom. "Hello Tom," she sang out.

Junior meowed a complaint at being left out, and she bent down and scratched his head. "Hello, Junior. How are you?" Junior rubbed his head against her hand.

She straightened back up, and I helped her take off the lightweight jacket she wore. "Where'd you go?" I asked.

"Oh, here and there, here and there." Barbara's face shone with a playful innocence that I didn't believe. "It's a beautiful day out there, did you know?" She headed for the back room, taking the scarf off her hair as she did. "Give me a minute, and I'll make us all some lunch," she called as she pushed through the beaded curtains.

Lynn and I looked at each other.

"Don't ask me," Lynn said. "I have no idea what she's up to."

Twenty-Nine

I admit it. I don't like guns. I don't like the way they look, I don't like the way they feel, and I certainly don't like what they can do to a person's body. When the man pushed back his suit coat to show me the pistol tucked into his waistband, I didn't argue. I let him take my elbow and guide me to a large, black sedan with tinted windows. A door swung open, and with a little prodding from my escort, I got in.

It was midmorning. I was walking east along Tenth Street, just past Walnut Avenue, when the man with the gun made his request that I join his boss in the car. He did it well. He had been waiting for me within the entrance of the vacant Woolworth's, probably watching in the reflection of the angled display window, much as I've waited for my own victims in the past.

A man sat on the far side of the back seat. It took me all of half a second to recognize him. Tall, thin, almost cadaverous, with long gray hair tied back in a thin ponytail. It was the man who'd shot Zager in the lobby of the Meridian Hotel. I did my best to keep from showing I recognized him and instead made a big deal of settling myself on the car seat. All the while he didn't say anything, he simply watched me.

It felt like he wasn't so much looking at me as he was studying me. It didn't make me feel any better about my situation.

"Mister Gregory Smith, I presume? The pickpocket known as The Kid?" The man's voice was honey smooth and cyanide sharp at the same time.

"Could be," I said, remembering I wasn't supposed to know him. "And you are?"

"That doesn't matter, Mr. Smith." He considered me for a little longer, then stared at the back of his hand and said, "I'm curious about something, Mr. Smith."

"What's that?"

He turned back to me. "How is it that a known thief such as yourself is allowed to walk around the city without worry of arrest? You don't even have a police record. It makes me wonder if perhaps you haven't, shall we say, friends in high places?"

"I don't have a record, and the police aren't after me because I'm good. I make it a point not to get caught."

"And yet I have caught you."

"Your guy grabbed me, but I have no idea why. I don't know you. I do know I never boosted your wallet."

"Your memory is that good?"

"Yes, it is." We glared at each other for a few moments and then he reached into his coat and brought out a billfold and handed it to me.

"Let's see how good your memory really is, Mr. Smith. Have you ever seen that wallet before?" I examined it. It was the wallet I'd lifted from Zager.

"You can't expect me to remember every wallet I've taken."

"Try, Mr. Smith."

I opened the billfold. It was empty. "It would help if the cards and stuff that were inside were still in there," I protested.

"Nonetheless, please try." I closed my eyes and made a show of feeling the wallet's texture, shape, size and heft, and then I nodded.

"A week ago, Thursday? In the lobby of the Meridian. He was walking toward the front doors, and I had just come in. I bumped him, got the wallet and left through the garage doors."

"And then," the man prompted.

"I walked a couple of blocks, took out the cards and cash and left the wallet in a trash bin at the corner of Division and Twelfth." That was the story Talbot, Cochran and I had worked out. In reality, they had arranged to have it turned in to the local police station and reported as having been found in that trash bin.

"Wasn't there something else in the wallet?"

"No, there wasn't." The man's face darkened, but before he could say anything I interrupted. "Wait, yes there was. It was a memory card, the kind you put into a camera. It was tucked down in the pocket."

"You didn't take it?"

I gave him a disdainful laugh. "No, that kind of thing doesn't have any value on the street."

There was a long silence. I wondered what his next move would be.

"Very well, Mr. Smith. I accept your version of events."

I raised an eyebrow at that. "Gee, that's really swell of you, whoever you are."

The back of his hand whacked my face. "I don't like smart alecks, Mr. Smith, nor do I like petty thieves. You appear to be both. Please get out of my car."

Someone must have been listening, because the door opened, and the same guy who had put me into the car pulled me out. He got in without glancing at me. The door closed again, and the car pulled away into the street.

I put my hand to my face and rubbed where he had hit me. It smarted like hell, but that was the least of my concerns. I called Cochran as soon as I was certain no one was tailing me.

"What's up, Kid? I'm in a meeting."

I told him what had happened. There was a long silence on the other end of the line when I finished. I suspected that Cochran was conferring with Talbot.

His first question when he came back on the line confirmed that. "Talbot wants to know if you are certain it was the same man who shot Zager."

I told him what I thought of Talbot's question. He translated my answer into a polite yes for Talbot, then he got back to me.

"Well, if there was any doubt before, we now know for certain that Wolfe's people believe you stole the wallet. Talbot said to tell you, good job."

I told Cochran what Talbot could do and where he could do it, and then I hung up. I headed back to The Book Nook, wondering how Cochran translated that.

Thirty

The invitation came in that day's mail. It came in the form of an elegant, off-white, square envelope. It was addressed to me in a careful calligraphic script and requested the pleasure of my company for lunch at The Empire Room. Doris had signed it with a flourish and then penned a postscript.

"I hope, My Dear Kid, that you will not disappoint me." The date specified for our lunch was the next day.

"Oh, hell," Sammie said when I showed it to him later that day. I was there to drop off another assortment of wallets. "Don't go, Kid. I've heard about these lunches of hers. There's only two ways you leave from them."

"And they are?"

"Through the front door, if you sign on the dotted line and agree to work for Doris."

"And the other?"

"Through the back door with your fingers broken, if you don't." Sammie handed the invitation back to me. "Don't go, Kid."

"The problem is that I have to keep up the appearance for at least a few more days until Talbot finishes up his operation."

Sammie grunted as he went over the figures on the tally sheet and then handed it to me. "I still don't trust that guy, Kid. I wish I'd never gotten mixed up with him. I prefer working with crooks. At least you know they're trying to rip you off."

I signed my name to the tally sheet while mentally adding the value of the stolen goods I'd turned over to Sammie. I gave a small whistle. "I didn't know I was on such a roll."

Sammie smiled. "I guess it's a good thing for the cops that you're on their side. Otherwise the news would be carrying stories about the latest crime wave."

Thirty-One

Sammie's words of warning still echoed in my head as I walked up the steps of The Empire Room and pushed my way through the lobby doors as if I owned the place. I figured a bold front was my best move, despite the lack of anything with which to back it up.

Although it was only a few minutes before eleven, I felt a bit like a western gunfighter meeting his adversary at noon for a showdown—except in my case, the middle of the street was a plush and ornate dining room where the sparkle of chandeliers competed with the sparkle of diamonds rings on so many of its patrons' fingers.

My illusion of control vanished in the length of time it took someone to jab something hard into my side that felt like I imagined a gun would feel. Jeremy and another of Doris's gang stood close beside me.

"Come on, Kid. This way." He jabbed me again, and I shuffled off with them. We crossed the wide lobby with them not letting me get more than a few inches away as we walked. There must have been a dozen people in the lobby, but no one paid attention as we pushed through a service door at the back.

Our journey continued down an industrial hallway whose last refurbishing had been when Eisenhower was president. A flight of black iron stairs brought us down to the open door of a boiler room.

The other guy felt my coat pockets until he found my cell phone. He showed it to Jeremy, who shoved it into his jacket pocket.

Jeremy shoved me inside the boiler room and slammed the door shut before I could catch my footing. I heard the doorknob rattle as he locked it.

I was alone.

I didn't shout.

I didn't pound on the door.

I admit to trying the doorknob.

I also paced a lot. The room was about twenty-five feet by fifteen. A large steam boiler took up most of the space. It was hot, and the air smelled of oil. A constant hiss of unseen steam and water was just loud enough to notice but not too loud to tune out.

As I paced the short open space on the floor, I made a list of the mistakes I had made in my life. This was near the top. I tried to look at my watch, but it wasn't there. Ever since I've been carrying a cell phone, I've haven't bothered to wear a watch very often.

I tried counting to a thousand as a way to mark time but was distracted somewhere around four-hundred and fifty by a mouse running across the floor. Mainly I just paced.

The door opened again after what I calculated to be four hours. Jeremy stood in the entrance.

"Come on," he said, echoing our previous conversation.

I stayed where I was and held up my hand. "Just one moment."

Jeremy looked puzzled. "What? You can't do that."

I put my fists on my hips. "Answer me one question, and I'll go with you."

He looked around as if I was trying to con him. Satisfied there were no lurking dangers, he said, "Okay. What's your question?"

"What time is it?"

He told me. Exactly two hours and ten minutes since I'd arrived. So much for my keen sense of time.

Thirty-Two

The lobby was empty of all but a few patrons. They took no notice as we left the service door and crossed the lobby. Jeremy opened one of the leather-paneled doors for me. I paused, and he gave me a little shove.

The dining room was at near capacity, and the air was filled with the low murmur of conversations, competing with the sound of the small grand piano near the entrance. The pianist was a short woman with blonde, spiked hair. She was dressed in black slacks, a matching black jacket and a starched white blouse. She smiled at me when she saw I was watching her, then turned back to the sheet music in front of her. It was an old Beatles song, gentrified by its arrangement and setting. I wondered if such music would accompany my fingers being broken.

Probably not, I decided. That would be done back in the boiler room so that my screams didn't disturb the diners and spoil their lunch.

Jeremy poked me. "Come on, Kid. Get going."

Doris Whitaker was at her usual table on the far side of the large room, and I wove my way through the tables to her. She looked me up and down and nodded as I arrived.

"How nice of you to accept my invitation, Kid, and that tie works very well with the shirt. Was that your choice, or did your wife Lynn pick it out for you?"

My heart grew cold at her words. Doris was making it clear that Lynn would be a target as well if I didn't go along. "Hello, Doris. Thank you for inviting me. May I?" I motioned to the empty chair opposite her.

The two who had grabbed me sat on either side. The one whose name I had yet to learn was on my left, and Jeremy on my right. I noticed both were keeping their chairs at a slight angle to the table. I guess Chad had warned them of what had happened last time.

I became aware of a pair of lengthy legs in fishnet stockings and stiletto heels standing next to me, and a waitress placed a salad in front of me along with a glass of iced tea. I should have thanked her, but under the circumstances my manners were diminished.

"I took the liberty of ordering for you," said Doris. "I hope you don't mind."

I picked up the iced tea and took a sip.

"Not at all, Doris." I put down my drink and picked up the salad fork. Start with the outside and work your way in, Fast Eddie had taught me all those years ago. I silently thanked his ghost for those years of etiquette lessons and tucked into the salad. If it was going to be the last meal I ate with unbroken fingers, then at least it was a good one. After a couple of bites I caught Doris studying me. "It's very good," I said, motioning toward the salad with the fork.

"Kid," said Doris. "I'm very disappointed in you. I thought you had better sense."

"Don't tell me I'm using the wrong fork after all," I replied with a cheerfulness I didn't feel.

Movement behind me stopped my thoughts. Chad had walked up behind me. This did not look good. "Hello, Chad," said Doris. "You're late. You know I don't like tardiness."

Chad answered her. "I'm sorry, Mrs. Whitaker. It took longer than I expected to get the information."

"And?"

Chad went around the table and leaned over to whisper to her.

I watched her eyes. She showed momentary surprise, and then her eyes grew cold. "I see. You did very well, Chad. Thank you."

Doris motioned to the guy on my left. "Gordon, go back downstairs and make certain everything is ready."

He got up and left, and Chad sat down in his place. Jeremy, on my other side, got up and stood next to me. I wasn't going to be able to duck out so fast this time.

Doris looked at me with regret. "I had so hoped we could work together, but now I see that it was never to be."

I swallowed. This was not going the way it was supposed to go. I started to protest. "Well, now, Doris, let's not give up completely on working together. Maybe we can work something out."

Doris shook her head. "Do you know what Chad just told me?"

It was my turn to shake my head.

"He told me he was late because he was checking out some information I've recently received."

"Information about what?"

"Information about you, Kid. That you are working for the feds and are helping them build a case against me."

I almost laughed with relief. "Oh, come on, Doris. You don't believe that, do you?"

"I have to admit I had my doubts."

I started to relax. Too soon, as it turned out.

"Chad, why don't you tell The Kid where you were this morning?"

We both turned to Chad, whose wolfish grin was working overtime.

He cracked his knuckles. "The man who gave Mrs. Whitaker the dope on you also told her how to confirm what he said. I went to your bookstore and handed a note to the old geezer behind the counter and told him to give it to Agent Cochran."

My heart felt as if it had stopped.

Chad continued. "The old guy went to the back room, and a minute later this other dude came out with the note." Doris motioned to him to continue.

Chad went on to describe how Cochran, confused by the note, which was blank inside, had come out from the back room and identified himself. Chad had excused himself and left.

I barely listened to what he was saying. All I knew was that I was in trouble, deep trouble.

I became aware that Chad's story had ended, and all three of them were looking at me. It was strange. I was sitting in a crowded, swank restaurant where people were talking and laughing and enjoying their meals and drinks. I was surrounded by people in a public place but was as alone as I've ever been in my life.

I made an effort to talk my way out of it. "It isn't what you think, Doris."

"Shut the hell up," Doris said with a snarl that exposed the woman under the façade. "If there's one thing I can't stand, it's a stool pigeon." She clasped her hands tight as though trying to control her emotion. After a few seconds she looked at Chad and then at Jeremy. "Are you boys up to what needs to be done, or should I do it?"

"Yeah, Mrs. Whitaker, I can do it," replied Chad.

Not to be left out, Jeremy bobbed his head up and down and said, "Me, too, Mrs. Whitaker."

Doris checked her tiny, elegant wristwatch and gave a quick glance around the restaurant.

"It's too crowded to get him out without creating a scene. We'll have to wait."

Something caught her eye behind me. "Shit, I forgot about your lunch."

A waitress arrived a few seconds later with a large silver platter carried above her head. Doris waved and awarded her a tight-lipped smile.

"I'm sorry, dear, but we aren't ready for our entrées just yet."

"Yes, Ma'am. I'll take these back to the kitchen." The waitress turned to go, but the huge tray got away from her, and an instant later Chad found himself with a lap full of food.

"You clumsy cow!" shouted Doris. The waitress took no notice and instead delivered a powerful kick with her fishnet-stockinged leg and drove a wickedly pointed, high-heeled shoe right into Jeremy's crotch. He doubled over and fell with a cry. Half a second later the waitress swiveled and brought the empty tray crashing down on Chad's head. He fell face forward onto the table. It was all over in no more than three seconds.

The waitress grabbed my shoulder. "Come on, Kid!" she shouted in a voice I love. I looked up at her from where I sat. Her blonde wig was askew, and I could see black hair under it.

"Lynn?"

She didn't answer. She just hauled me to my feet and gave me a kiss.

I tossed my napkin on the table in front of Doris. She had a dazed look on her face. "Sorry, Doris, got to run."

I took a few precious seconds to grab my cell phone from Jeremy's jacket.

"Come on, Kid, let's get out of here!" Lynn tugged on my arm.

She and I joined hands and ran out of the Empire Room, past bewildered patrons and staff alike. As we ran past the pianist near the door, she gave us a mock salute, then continued playing.

Lynn paused in the lobby long enough to take off her shoes. "I can run faster without them."

We kept on running out the front doors and down the steps to where a car was waiting. Lynn opened the back door, and we piled in. Cochran was behind the wheel. He punched the gas, the tires squealed, and we took off.

Thirty-Three

I was angry, and it scared me how angry I was.

Lynn squeezed my hand. "Kid," she said in a voice that showed she was scared of my anger, as well. "You've got to calm down."

She looked at Cochran. "Cochran's right. We don't know for certain Talbot's the one who told Doris that he was here at the store."

It had been less than an hour since my narrow escape from The Empire Room, but it was more than enough time for my anger to build.

"Who else could have told her?" I demanded of Cochran yet again as we sat at the table in the back room.

He didn't answer this time, knowing nothing he had said so far or could say would satisfy me.

The buzzing of Cochran's cell phone broke the silence. He flipped it open and mouthed the name of the caller, "Talbot." Then he answered.

Lynn and I listened as he gave his boss a condensed version of what had happened. Talbot must not have responded right away, as after a long pause Cochran asked, "Are you still there?" A moment later he added, "Yes, both Greg and Lynn are here with me."

He lowered the cell phone from his ear, placed it on the table and pressed a button. "Okay, we're on speaker phone."

"Smith? Talbot here. I understand you ran into some difficulty."

My face grew hot. "Yes, I suppose you could call almost being killed some difficulty."

"Well, I'm glad things worked out okay. Ms. Vargas, Cochran says you saved the day. Nice work."

I was about to begin my hour-in-preparation tirade when Lynn squeezed my hand again.

"Not now, Kid," she said. "Let Cochran talk."

I didn't want to, but I did as she asked.

Cochran shot her a grateful look and then spoke. "Talbot, The Kid and Ms. Vargas are wondering how Doris Whitaker learned that I have been staying at The Book Nook."

"Oh, they are, are they?"

"Yes, and frankly, I am too. This shouldn't have happened. I'd like permission to investigate."

There was another long pause at the other end.

Talbot finally ended it by saying, "You are right, it shouldn't have happened. Look, I've got to run. Let me check out a few things before you go any further on this, okay?"

He hung up before Cochran could reply.

Cochran got to his feet. "Something's not right about this," he said as he put his cell phone back into his pocket. He glanced at the clock. It was just going on three. "I'm going out for a while, should be back by dinner. Stick around the store, will you?"

"What if Chad and Jeremy decide to pay a visit?" I asked.

"They won't."

"Why not?"

He gave a wry smile. "Because now they know I'm here," he made the sign of quotation marks in the air with his fingers, "protecting you."

"He's right," said Lynn in surprise.

"Well, I guess it's an ill wind and all that," I said, agreeing. We watched him leave, noting the worry marking his young face.

I listened to the beaded curtain behind me, swinging widely, the strands clicking against each other in the first seconds after he left, then slowing and finally stopping . "What do you think?" I asked Lynn, studying her face.

"I think," she replied after a long moment, "that Cochran has some doubts about Talbot, and I agree."

Thirty-Four

In spite of the turmoil around us, Lynn and I couldn't ignore the day-to-day demands of life. She had dance classes to teach, and so she headed upstairs to change into her leotard and get the studio ready for the first hordes of children coming for their after-school lessons. I had bookstore duties to occupy my time. It's amazing how many mundane tasks are necessary in running a small business.

Several hours later I was up at the front of the store, straightening and shelving books and watching the front counter. I had calmed down considerably since our conversation, if you can call it that, with Talbot.

The bell over the door chimed. It was Barbara, coming in after yet another afternoon spent doing whatever mysterious task she was doing.

"Hello, Kid!" she called as she took off her coat.

She looked tired. I tried again to find out what she was up to but to no avail.

"Sorry, Kid. This is something I have to take care of myself." She gave me a hug. "Thank you, though. I'll let you know if you can help." She disappeared into the back room.

Old Tom arrived a little while later at six p.m. As if on cue my cell phone rang.

It was Cochran.

"Kid, I think I need some help. Can you come meet me?" His voice was calm, almost flat.

"What's up, Cochran? Where are you?"

He gave me the name of a hotel nearby. "Room 421. Call me when you are in the lobby." He hung up before I could ask any more questions.

I left Old Tom watching the front and went into the back room and told Barbara I was going out to meet Cochran. Lynn came down the stairs as I finished, and I had to explain the odd telephone call again.

"Do you think it's safe?" she asked.

"He didn't give any sign of there being trouble," I told her with a confidence I lacked, then gave her a quick kiss and left.

The Broadmore Hotel was only a few blocks away, and I walked them quickly through the rush hour traffic of vehicles on the street and office workers crowding the sidewalks.

I took out my cell phone as I entered the lobby and called Cochran. He answered on the first ring.

"I'm in the lobby and heading for the elevator," I told him.

He gave a quick acknowledgment and hung up. I took the elevator to the fourth floor.

The elevator opened onto a hallway that was like any hallway in any high-priced hotel in the country. The thick carpet muffled my footsteps as I passed a series of doors. One door opened just as I was passing. A young woman clutched a purse and coat tightly, and she hurried past me and down the hall the way I had come, toward the elevators. A man had been standing behind her, and he closed it but only after giving me a defiant look as though daring me to say something. I ignored him and went on down the hallway.

I knocked on the door of suite 421. "Cochran? It's me, The Kid," I said in a low voice.

The door opened. Cochran grabbed my arm, hurried me inside and closed the door behind us.

We were in a modest-sized room with a sofa and two chairs, a writing desk and a wet bar on one side. A set of closed curtains hid what I supposed were floo-to-ceiling windows looking out over the city. There was a door in the wall to our left, next to the sofa. It was closed. Cochran's face was pale.

"What's going on?" I asked.

He pointed toward the door. "Talbot's in the bedroom. He's dead."

Thirty-Five

Talbot lay on his back on the bed in the next room. He was dressed as I was used to seeing him, in a business suit and tie, but his coat was off, hanging from the back of a chair near the wardrobe. The front of his shirt was stained with blood. To my unpracticed eye it looked like he had been shot in the heart. I sniffed the air. There was a copper smell from the blood as well as a trace of gunpowder—no surprise there.

Cochran stood behind me. "That's how I found him twenty minutes ago."

"Have you called the police?"

"No, not yet. I was hoping you'd call your buddy, Lieutenant Johnston."

Mel's an old friend of mine, despite being on the job. He's a homicide cop and a good one. I took out my cell phone, found his number, called him and explained the situation.

"He'll be here with a team in ten minutes." I told Cochran after I hung up.

He avoided my eyes and went back into the living room and sat down in one of the easy chairs. I followed him and sat in the other.

"Any other reason you didn't call the cops?"

He looked at me with a trace of a smile. "You mean, did I kill him?"

I kept my eyes on his but didn't answer.

He held my gaze for a few seconds, then looked toward the bedroom where Talbot's body lay. "No, Kid, I didn't. But I could have."

I asked him what he meant.

"When I got here the first time, Talbot was alive. We talked for at least fifteen minutes. He was just as upset as you and I were that Doris Whitaker knows about me."

"Yeah, I bet."

"No, really, he was. Apparently he had told his mole in Wofe's organization, and the mole told Wolfe. Talbot figured Wolfe had to be the one who leaked the information to her."

"You said the first time you got here."

"Yes. We talked for a few minutes, and then he got a call on his cell phone and told me I had to leave for a few minutes. It was obvious he didn't want me to hear what he said. He told me he would call my cell phone when I could come back."

"So you left him here alive?"

"I went down the hallway and around the corner and waited. I was able to use the reflection in a window at the end of the hallway to see the entire length of it. I saw a man come from the elevators and go to Talbot's door, knock and go inside. A few minutes later the man left."

"You didn't recognize him?"

"No, I couldn't see any details in the reflection." He took a breath and continued. "I waited the fifteen minutes and then fifteen minutes more. I went back to Talbot's room, but he didn't answer the door, and he didn't answer his cell phone either. So I got the maid to let me in."

"How did you do that?"

"I'd been staying here myself up until a couple of days ago, remember?"

I nodded.

He continued. "I simply showed my ID to one of the maids. She remembered seeing me and Talbot together often enough that she didn't think it strange I'd need to get into his suite."

"And you found him like that?"

"Yes." Cochran appeared calm enough, but I noticed his fingers lightly drumming on his knee, and he was biting his lip.

"There's more, isn't there?"

Cochran cast a glance to both sides before answering. "The thing is, I know who the mole in Wolfe's organization is."

Thirty-Six

Mel arrived in eight minutes, not ten. He greeted Cochran and me and shook his head. "I'd like to say it's good to see you again, Agent Cochran, but under the circumstances I don't think I can." He raised his hand, holding two fingers next to each other. "You do know that I'm this close to retiring, don't you? I don't need another messy case like last time."

Mel and I go way back to when I was a street-wise teenager and he was street cop trying to keep kids like me out of trouble. Fortunately for me, our paths never crossed in a professional way, at least not until last year.

His team arrived just then, and he sent them into the bedroom to begin their evidence gathering. Mel took Cochran and me out into the hallway, where I let Cochran tell his story again. When he got to the part about seeing the man arrive and then leave, Mel asked him to wait for a minute while he sent someone down to the hotel office to see about securing a copy of any surveillance video they might have.

That done, he turned his attention back to us. "Agent Cochran, are you armed?"

Cochran nodded and removed a pistol from a shoulder holster. He handed it butt-first to Mel.

Mel accepted it and sniffed the barrel. "Clean," he said, as he handed it back

Cochran put it back into its holster.

"Your men will find that Talbot's gun hasn't been fired either."

"You touched it?"

"No, just gave it the sniff test."

Mel sent us back to The Book Nook after a few more questions. "Why am I not surprised?" he said when learning that Cochran was staying there. He told us he'd stop by later in the evening.

A policewoman passed us as we were leaving. She carried a sheaf of printed photographs.

Cochran stopped her and called to Mel, "Lieutenant Johnston, may I take a copy of this?

Mel waved his agreement, and Cochran accepted a copy. He barely glanced at it before handing it to me. "Who else would it be?"

The photo, a screen grab from surveillance tape, showed a tall, thin man with a tight ponytail. Though his face was not completely visible, I had no doubt of his identity. It was the man who'd killed Zager as I picked his pocket.

As we left the hotel Cochran suggested we stop and pick up a couple of cups of coffee. I suspect he could have used something stronger but didn't mention it. A few minutes later, with both of us sipping from paper cups, we walked over to a bench on the square and sat down.

Cochran took out his cell phone and called someone. He turned his head away as he spoke, but I had a pretty good idea who he had called. When he was done he put away his phone, then sat without talking.

That didn't bother me. I had a lot of thoughts going through my mind, as well. I waited for Cochran to decide when and what he was going to say.

"That was Riley," Cochran said. "He says there's a special investigation team arriving in a few hours." He glanced at his watch. "I'll pick them up late tonight at the airport."

"A special team?"

"The murder of an agent gets pretty high priority." He fell silent again.

I checked the action around the square. It was getting chilly as the evening drew near. Aside from a couple of homeless people wrapped in blankets, we were the only ones using the benches. Everyone else was in a hurry to get someplace. I slipped the paper sleeve off my coffee cup and warmed my hands on the cup.

Cochran turned to me. "I never liked Talbot. He was an ambitious bastard who didn't care who he hurt as he moved up the ladder at the agency."

I didn't reply, and after a pause he continued. "Still, I was working for him on this assignment. He was my boss, and someone killed him." His eyes pleaded for understanding. "I've got to help them do whatever it takes to find who killed him."

"Regardless of who gets hurt in the process?" I was thinking of the warrant for Barbara that Talbot had.

Cochran nodded. "I know there's no chance of a connection between Barbara and this, but I won't be handling the investigation. The team that's arriving tonight will look through his files, and they'll find that warrant." We returned to nursing our coffees, neither willing to give voice to our concern.

I changed the subject. "Back at the hotel you said you knew who Talbot's mole is in Wolfe's organization."

"Talbot told me when I arrived. Believe me, Kid, he was just as worried as we were that Doris Whitaker had found about you helping us. That's when he told me. The mole is Dennis Metcalf, Wolfe's lawyer."

"His own lawyer? Isn't there some kind of rule about client confidence and all that?"

"Ordinarily, yes, but a lawyer is also an officer of the court and duty bound to report knowledge of a crime. Not that Metcalf is operating out of any sense of civic duty."

"Oh?"

"No, Talbot cut a deal with Metcalf. Full immunity for any crimes he may have committed while working for Wolfe in exchange for all the details on Wolfe's operations."

"Sounds like a sweet deal for both Metcalf and Talbot."

"Yeah, up until now. Wolfe must have found out about Metcalf's deal with Talbot. Talbot told me the data card that was supposed to be in the courier's wallet was the last bit of confirming evidence, tying all of Wolfe's activities and accounts together."

"No wonder Talbot was so eager to get his hands on it."

Cochran nodded. "Riley suggested I pay Metcalf a visit. He's staying at The Meridian. I gave him a call, and he told me to come over." Cochran eyed me.

"And?" I asked.

"I'm thinking I'd like you to come along, too."

"Why me?"

Cochran shrugged his shoulders. "Kid, I'm foundering in the dark here. I don't know which way is up or who I can trust. I'd like you to hear what he has to say and how he says it. We can compare notes afterward and decide if he's on the up and up."

I had to agree that it made sense. Besides, I was tired of always being one step behind events.

Cochran took the top off his coffee and drained what was left. I did the same as we got up from the bench and began walking back to Metcalf's hotel, pitching our empty cups in a wastebasket as we left the square.

Thirty-Seven

Metcalf's suite was on the top floor of the hotel as befitted, if not a captain of industry, then the lawyer of a captain of industry. Cochran and I approached the car at the end of the bank of elevators, the one with a prominent sign that read Penthouse Floor Only. A uniformed elevator operator asked our names, then ushered us in after we provided them. He pushed the single button with one white-gloved finger. We ascended to the twelfth floor in silence. When the doors opened the operator accompanied us down the hallway. We stopped in front of suite 310, and the elevator operator knocked discreetly.

A few seconds later the door opened, and a tall, aristocratic looking man took a look at Cochran and me, then said to the operator, "Thank you, Louis." The elevator operator nodded and left. Metcalf opened the door wider and motioned to us to come inside.

I have to admit, I had never been inside a penthouse suite before, and at first its opulence and crass ostentation made me speechless. I knew people, Mel and Alice Johnston, for example, whose entire house held less square footage than this penthouse suite.

We were in the foyer. A large living room lay in front of us while two hallways, one on each side, led to what I assumed were bedrooms. Our host walked past us into the living room, and we followed. There was a wide fireplace against one wall and a wet bar against another. I spotted a doorway next to the bar and could see a galley kitchen through it.

But it was the patio outside the floor-to-ceiling sliding doors that struck me the most. The patio was easily forty or more feet square with sets of tables and chairs scattered about. I could see a fire pit and at least a dozen potted plants and small trees. Near the doors was a short putting green with a bag of golf clubs lying next to it. Beyond the edge of the patio, the city stretched out to the bay and its opposite shore like a painted backdrop.

My fascination with the view must have amused our host. "Would you care to step outside for a minute?" he asked with the boredom of a host trying to be gracious to someone he believes beneath his social class. Much as I hated to admit it, I did.

Metcalf walked over to the sliding door, opened it with an easy motion and stepped out onto the patio, not waiting or looking to see if I followed. The sixth-grader in me was tempted to slide the door closed behind him and lock it, but my grownup self followed him outside.

I squinted in the afternoon sun as a breeze brushed past my face and ruffled my hair. I heard the sound of traffic twelve stories below. Above our heads a jet growled as it passed in the distance, and a few birds gave throat. I took a deep breath and tasted the air. The scents of the city were still present but overshadowed by the smell of salt and sea from the bay.

Metcalf walked over to the low parapet that ran around the edge of the building, turned on his heel, and faced me with his arms wide. "What do you think, Mr. Smith? Worth a few thousand a day, don't you think?"

I gave an uncommitted response and went back inside. This time it was Metcalf who followed me.

He closed the door and gestured to a set of chairs. "Shall we, gentlemen?" Once we were seated, Metcalf lost much of the confidence he'd portrayed minutes before.

"Agent Talbot's death came as quite a shock, Agent Cochran," he confessed. "I have to tell you that it causes me to doubt your agency's ability to provide the protection from Wofe I was promised."

Cochran spent the next few minutes trying to assure Metcalf that he would be well protected. I had to wonder myself how safe he really was, but it seemed to mollify him. Then Cochran switched gears. He dropped the photograph from the surveillance video on the coffee table. "Do you recognize this man?"

The effect on Metcalf was immediate. His face grew pale, and even though we were cocooned within his luxury hotel suite, he looked around as if expecting to see gunmen in every corner. "Well?" asked Cochran.

Metcalf swallowed. "Yes, I know him, or at least I know who he is." He pursed his lips. "I've met him only once, that was at Wolfe's estate on the island."

He explained how he had just arrived for one of his monthly meetings with Wolfe, and it seemed the man in the photograph was just leaving. They passed each other in the doorway of Wolfe's study. When Metcalf asked Wolfe about him, he told him the man was a fixer. "He told me Newcomb, that was the man's name, and I are in the same business. I fix things via the law of the land, while Newcomb fixes things via the law of the jungle."

Metcalf took a moment to gaze at the view outside the patio doors and then continued. "He left me no doubt as to the type of work Newcomb does." His voice betrayed his worry.

"The impression you received was correct," agreed Cochran. "Loren Newcomb is a professional hit man, one of the best and most expensive. His nickname is The Deacon."

Cochran turned to me. "He's also the one who killed Zager, Wolfe's currier."

Metcalf held up a hand. "Please, Agent Cochran. Until that letter of immunity is signed, sealed and delivered, I will not comment on any possible legal transgressions my client, Mister Wolfe, may or may not have committed."

Metcalf probably meant that to be a close to our conversation, but I wasn't ready to let that happen.

I turned to Cochran. "There's another matter we need to discuss, isn't there, Cochran?" My anger about Doris Whitaker finding out about my arrangement with Talbot was building again.

He nodded. "Mr. Metcalf, Agent Talbot told of Mr. Smith's role, didn't he?"

"You mean that he's a pickpocket Talbot recruited to take Zager's wallet?"

Cochran nodded.

Metcalf took an interest in his fingernails. "Yes, he told me, why?"

I banged a fist on the coffee table. As there were no coffee cups on it, and also as it was made of heavy glass and steel, there was only a quiet thud and a pain in my hand, not the effect I wanted.

"Because someone told Doris Whitaker, that's why."

"Doris Whitaker?" The name drew a blank with Metcalf.

"She's the leader of the largest pickpocketing gang in the city," explained Cochran. "She erroneously thinks that The Kid, Mr. Smith was working with us in an effort to build a case against her."

"Well, that's ridiculous." He looked at me with some of his old disdain returning. "I have no knowledge of this Mrs. Whitaker nor of any other pickpockets in this town." He sniffed. "And I wish to God I didn't know you." He got up. "If you'll excuse me gentlemen, I have an appointment in court in an hour for which I cannot be late."

We stood and said our goodbyes and left.

We didn't talk in the elevator going back down, the operator's presence precluded that, but as soon as we made the lobby, we both spoke at the same time.

"What do you think?" Cochran asked as I asked him the same question. Cochran answered first.

"I think he's scared. The photograph of that hit man of Wolfe's really shook him."

"The hell with that," I said. "What about Doris? Do you think he tipped her off?" Cochran shook his head.

"I don't see why. What would he gain by doing that? My guess is she heard it elsewhere on the street. I was probably seen going into The Book Nook by someone who recognized me as an FBI agent."

We parted company at the corner of Market and Oak. Cochran had to meet yet again with the team investigating Talbot's murder while I had books to shelve.

All in all, I think I had the better deal.

Thirty-Eight

As promised, Mel came by the bookstore that evening. He and Barbara greeted each other with big hugs. They go back together to the days when Mel was a cop on the beat and Barbara's store a hotbed of protest organizers. As a cop on street patrol back then, Mel was on the other side of the barricades, but during his off-hours he was a welcome worker at Barbara's shop. He took a long look at the kitchen when he came in.

"I remember when that wall over there was stacked this high with protest signs nailed to sticks of wood."

Barbara handed him a cup of tea. "Yes, and you were over there on the floor, nailing the signs to the sticks," she said with a smile. "If you look, you'll see there are still dents in the linoleum from your hammer."

Mel walked over and squatted down. He ran one of his big hands over the floor and nodded. Junior took advantage of his position and strolled over so that Mel could have the honor of giving him a quick bit of petting.

We sat at the table once more, Lynn, Barbara, Mel and me. Cochran was gone, heading to the airport to meet the investigating team due in from Washington. Max and April were out at a book signing.

"Kid," said Mel, getting down to business. "The chief is turning the investigation of Special Agent Talbot's death over to the feds at their request. I offered to hand our side of it over to someone else in the department, given our friendship, but she said it's not necessary, given that the feds are taking full charge."

He stopped to take a sip of tea. "I don't think you'll be bothered much, based on Cochran's statement that you didn't arrive until after he found Talbot's body."

Then his face grew stern. "What I want to know, Kid, is what's this I've heard about you going back to working the street as a pickpocket? One of the guys from the robbery detail gave me that bit of news this afternoon."

I told Mel about the operation Talbot and Cochran were running and how, after trying to teach Cochran how to pickpocket, I'd stepped in to do it.

Mel shook his head. "I can't believe they talked you into doing it, Kid. Do you have any idea of the risk you are running? Just because a fed gives you a get-out-of-jail-free card doesn't mean the district attorney is going to respect it."

It fell upon me to tell Mel about the hold Talbot had on Barbara. "Talbot had a warrant for Barbara's arrest. He was holding it over our heads. That's how he got me to agree to pretend to go back to picking pockets."

"You've got to be kidding."

We took turns explaining to Mel about James LeCuyer and the missing bank money from decades ago, as well as Talbot's blackmail.

When we were done, he shook his head. "Well, with your cover blown, at least that part's over."

"That's what we hope," said Lynn. "Unfortunately, it's already created trouble, and we're not certain what to do about it." We again took turns explaining how Doris Whitaker and her crew were on the warpath, believing me to be working with the local cops to bust her.

I had the fun of telling Mel about how Lynn rescued me from The Empire Room.

Mel studied Lynn with an amused smile. "Fishnet stockings, high heels and a short skirt, eh?"

Lynn stuck her tongue out at him. "Go ahead and picture it in your mind, 'cause that's the last time anyone will ever see me in a getup like that." Her face became serious. "Mel, isn't there anything you can do about Doris?"

Mel thought about it. "I'll have a word with the robbery division. I know she's been a thorn in the side of the department for years, but we've never been able to get anything on Doris herself, only the people working for her, and they're too intimidated to testify against her."

Mel stayed until close to eleven, chatting and catching up with us. Shortly after he left, Max and April came back. We all called out "Good night," to Tom out front and headed up the stairs to our respective rooms.

Cochran came back around midnight. Lynn and I heard his feet on the stairs and as he proceeded down the hallway. He stopped outside our door and knocked softly. "Kid, Lynn, are you awake?"

"Come in," I called.

He opened the door. Lynn switched on her bedside lamp, and we propped ourselves up on our pillows. Cochran stepped in. His face reddened when he saw us in bed.

"I'm sorry, I should have known you'd be asleep."

"No problem," I said. "What's up with the team you had to meet? Did they arrive safe and sound?"

"Yes. They'd like the three of us to meet with them in the morning. We'll meet them at their hotel at nine."

Lynn stifled a yawn. "Me, too?"

Cochran saw Lynn's bare shoulders and long black hair cascading on her pillow, and he looked away quickly. Lynn smiled.

"Yes, you too," he answered. "Apparently Special Agent Riley briefed them before they left, and he spoke highly of your opinion on things."

"What, and you don't share that opinion?" Lynn teased.

"No, I mean yes. I mean," he took a breath, "I share his regard."

Lynn laughed at his discomfort and a second later threw a pillow, my pillow, at him. My head clunked against the headboard.

"Hey!" I shouted. I grabbed Lynn's pillow out from under her. Cochran took advantage of our horseplay to make his escape, closing our bedroom door behind him.

Thirty-Nine

Lynn, Cochran and I walked to The Broadmore the next morning. I was tempted to ask Cochran about the advisability of the agents investigating Talbot's death staying in the same hotel in which he was murdered, but I decided against it. He might not have appreciated the humor.

The morning fall mists were still rising from the streets, and the scent of the night still lingered as we strolled down Knickerbocker Lane. Shops were opening their doors and setting out tables of sale items on the sidewalk. We had enough time that we were able to stop and chat with our neighbors, to compliment an attractive window display, to commiserate on a drop in business.

The two FBI agents were waiting in the hotel lobby when we arrived. Both men resembled a television director's image of what an FBI agent should look like. They were both tall, broad shouldered and, as far as I could tell, devoid of any sense of humor. One introduced himself as Special Agent Cranz. The other was Special Agent Stern. I can't say with certainty that I knew which was which, and I doubt that would have mattered to either of them.

The manager of The Broadmore had made a conference room on the second floor available. The five of us walked up the broad staircase to the mezzanine level and down a hall to the conference room. It was a room more befitting an executive board meeting than an interview with two steely-eyed federal agents. The table could easily sit a dozen people, and there was a pitcher of ice water and glasses on a credenza off to one side. The air had a sterile taste, as though The Broadmore staff disinfected the room after each use.

Cochran excused himself at the doorway, saying he needed to go to the federal building and write a report. The door closed behind him, and Lynn and I accepted an invitation to sit down and be comfortable, not an easy thing to do under the circumstances.

Once we were settled and introductions were made, Agent Cranz or Agent Stern asked me to tell them how I had gone to the Hotel Broadmore at Cochran's request, and what I found there. It was apparent they were operating under instructions not to press too hard on my role in Talbot's operation, though they did ask Lynn and me quite a few questions, in a roundabout way, about what we thought of Agent Talbot.

We gave our honest opinion but had to temper what we said, as we didn't want to draw their attention to Barbara's arrest warrant. I was still hoping they wouldn't find it.

Then they switched gears on us.

"Why did you call Lieutenant Johnston on discovering the Agent Talbot's body? What is your relationship with him?" asked Agent Cranz or maybe Agent Stern.

I explained how I had known Mel for years, and since he also knew Cochran, it would make sense to call him. That prompted more questions about our past history with Mel and Cochran.

"Maybe you ought to talk to Mel yourself," I suggested after a while.

"We will be doing that this afternoon," came the laconic reply followed by yet more questions.

The interview finished two hours later. I didn't know if they'd gleaned any useful information from us. I certainly didn't feel as though I'd learned anything except that Cranz and Stern were masters at keeping their thoughts hidden.

"We will be in touch if we have more questions," Agent Stern, I think, said as he closed the conference room door behind us.

Lynn and I gladly took our leave of The Broadmore and headed back home, rehashing the interview as we walked, with neither of us certain how it had gone.

Forty

The Book Nook was in total confusion when Lynn and I returned. Book displays were shoved to the sides, and the two armchairs had been moved up against the bookshelves along the back wall, blocking half the books on them. Stage lights and a couple of video cameras on tripods were aimed at the chairs, and a dozen people milled around looking as if they were doing something terribly important without actually doing anything.

Max Carson sat in one of the armchairs, the center of all the activity, looking as contented as a cat in sunshine and basking in the light of attention.

"Max!" I shouted. "What the hell is going on?"

The room became quiet as everyone looked at Lynn and me. A woman with a pinched face and a pen behind her ear hurried over to me.

"Sir, I'm afraid you'll have to leave. We're shooting a segment in just a few minutes."

I stared at her, then at Lynn and then around the room. The curtain to the back room parted, and Candy came in, holding Junior in her arms.

"Here he is, Max. He's all ready for his close up." She saw us and gave a squeal of delight. "Lynn! Kid! Isn't this great? I got Channel Five to do their interview with Max right here in The Book Nook. It'll be great publicity."

She carried Junior over to Max and placed him in his lap. I expected Junior to take off, but he surprised me by allowing Max to scratch his ears and was soon settled in the Great Author's lap.

Max gave me a broad smile. It was the smile of someone who has set you up for a practical joke that worked exactly right.

Candy explained to the pinch-faced woman, whose name was Vicky-the-Line-Producer, that Lynn and I were the owners of the store.

Vickie didn't seem impressed. "Perhaps there's someplace else where you can wait until we're done? Maybe you can go out for an early lunch?" She checked a sparkly watch on her wrist and saw the time. "Okay, brunch. Maybe you can go out for brunch." She held up her wrist so we could see the time. "We're on a very tight schedule here."

I shocked Lynn with the enthusiasm with which I greeted Vicky. Max was watching, too, his eyebrow cocked in puzzlement at my antics.

"I'm very pleased to meet you," I gushed to Vicky and insisted on shaking her hand, both her hands, with enthusiasm. "I just love watching Channel Five and am thrilled at having you here. *Mi casa es su casa.*"

That puzzled her.

"My store is your store," I told her.

Vicky freed herself from my grip, eyeing me with some wonder. "Thank you, Mister Smith. Now if you'll excuse us, we'll get back to work."

I took Lynn's arm and hustled her toward the doorway to the back room. We passed the chair where Max was holding Junior, and I held up my hand as though waving at him.

Max looked at my hand and let out a loud guffaw as we passed through the curtain and escaped into the back room.

Lynn shook free of my arm as soon as we were through the curtain and glared at me. "Why on earth did you let her get away with that, and what was Max laughing about?"

I opened my hand and showed her Vicky-the-Line-Producer's sparkly wristwatch.

Lynn tried, but she couldn't help laughing. "Oh, Kid. Okay, this time I forgive you, but you will give it back, won't you?"

A young woman with the television crew passed us, carrying a tray with cups of coffee on it. Lynn stopped her and asked her if she knew how long the interview would take. Lynn kept her distracted while I picked up a cup from the tray and slipped the watch around it. When she started to leave I pointed to the cup with the watch.

Her eyes widened.

"Make certain Vicky gets this cup first," I told her and sent her on her way.

The back room was almost as crowded as the front of the store. A well-dressed Asian woman sat at the table, where two other women worked on her hair and makeup. She was familiar, and I realized I had seen her on television, reporting on local stories. Over by the kitchen counter I saw April Quist sitting on a kitchen stool. She was paging through a notebook, studying it intently.

Lynn and I went over to her, the only person we knew in our own crowded kitchen.

"Hi, Lynn," she said and then added as almost an afterthought, "Hi, Kid."

Lynn squeezed my wrist, and I got the message. "If you two will excuse me," I said, "I've got some work to do upstairs."

Once upstairs, I wandered from room to room, wondering what it was I had to do up there. Soon I found myself in the room where I had set up the dressmaker's dummy for practicing. I went over to it and straightened the jacket hanging on it.

I idly slipped my hand into the pockets, one after the other, picking up a billfold from one, dropping it into another, without really thinking about it. Instead I found myself thinking about all the pockets I've picked in my life, all the lives I'd touched. I realized that every pocket I picked was like casting little pebbles into a lake, each with its own set of ripples spreading outward and each ripple disturbing the surface long after the pebble disappeared.

"I thought I'd find you up here," Lynn said from the doorway.

"What did April want?"

Lynn smiled as she came over and stood next to me. "She was showing me the notes she's been making about the girls who work at The Poodle. She's really interested in their stories."

My eyebrows went up. "I wonder if Max minds his assistant spending her time on things other than him?"

"I don't think Max has to worry about someone spending time on him."

"What do you mean?"

Lynn smiled at my naivety. "Kid, haven't you noticed how much time Candy has been spending here since Max moved in?"

I shook my head. I had no idea what Candy saw in him, but it reminded me of something else. "Speaking of which, when the heck is Max moving out? Hasn't Donnie been able to square things with Dom DeMarco yet?"

Lynn had the grace to look embarrassed. "Well, the fact is, that got taken care of right away. Max made an appearance at a book club Dom's wife belongs to, and everyone is happy."

"When did this happen? Why's he still here?"

"The thing is, Kid, Max likes it here, helping out behind the counter, meeting customers. And," she added, "it's been good for business, you've got to admit." She had a point. "Come on, Kid." She tugged on my hand. "The television crew should be wrapping up by now. Let's go downstairs."

Forty-One

It was my turn to make supper. Since it was fall, I elected to make a large batch of turkey chili with butternut squash. I prepared it early in the afternoon and tended it while catching up on the bookstore paperwork. The chili simmered on the stove all afternoon and filled the kitchen with its autumnal aroma. My timing was right for once, and both the chili and a pan of cornbread were ready when supper was called.

The table was comfortably crowded with Lynn, Barbara, me, Cochran and Max. Junior was having a bite of supper from his food dish. April had gone back to The Pink Poodle with Candy with no set time to return.

Max expressed his admiration for at least the tenth time at the way I had lifted Vicky's watch that afternoon. "Hell, Cochran, you should have seen how smooth he was. I was watching him the whole time and didn't see a thing."

Cochran began telling Max about the techniques I had tried to teach him.

There was a quiet knocking at the back door. Cochran stopped mid-sentence while we all looked at each other. That door opens onto an alley where the garbage bins are kept. During the day we receive shipments of books, but never at night. The knocking came again, even quieter than before.

Cochran and I got to our feet.

"Can you see who it is without opening the door?" Cochran asked in a low voice.

"No," I answered, matching his tone of voice.

He brought his pistol out from under his jacket and worked the slide. I didn't like the sound it made.

From the look on her face, Barbara didn't like the sound either, but Lynn put a finger to her own lips, and she got the message.

Max was already near the door, holding his walking stick over his shoulder. For a big, boisterous guy he could move like a cat when he wanted to.

Cochran took up a position facing the door, his pistol pointed down. I switched off the light and went to the door and, with Max next to me, pulled back the deadbolt, opened the door, and stepped back to one side.

A large figure stumbled in and said in a hoarse voice, "Shut the door, quick."

Max brought the door closed and threw the deadbolt. I flipped the light switch, and we viewed our visitor.

It was Joey. His clothes were disheveled, and there were bruises on his face. His knuckles were scraped and bleeding, and his wrists were tied together with twine.

Max and Cochran helped him to a chair while I grabbed a knife from a drawer and cut the string. Lynn brought a couple of wet washcloths from the sink and placed them on his wrists.

Barbara offered him a tiny glass with an amber liquid in it. Joey accepted it, downed it in one shot and then grimaced.

"Jeeze, what is that stuff?" he gasped.

Barbara took the glass back from him. "It's apricot cordial. I make it myself." She took the glass over to the sink and rinsed it. "We usually just sip it," she added.

Lynn brought over a bowl of chili, a couple of slices of cornbread on a plate, and a bottle of beer. Joey accepted it gratefully and dug in. He ate so fast that his bowl was clear before we could ask him any questions. "Any chance I can get some more of that?"

Lynn smiled. "Of course, coming right up."

This was our chance, and we took advantage of it. As Lynn took his bowl over to the stove to refill it, I asked, "So what happened, Joey?"

Joey took a long swallow of beer and launched into his story.

The car we had seen take him away had driven him to a house outside of town. There was a man waiting there who asked Joey if he had the data card Zager had been carrying.

At that point Joey stopped to open another bottle of beer. He seemed surprised to see the looks on our faces. "I told him I didn't have it, but he kept asking, like he didn't believe me."

"So then what happened?" asked Max. "How'd you get all those scrapes and bruises?"

"And who tied your hands?" chimed in Barbara.

"The same guys who took me to that house," answered Joey. He went on to explain, between spoonfuls of chili, what had happened next to him.

He was locked in a bedroom in the house. His captors brought him food twice a day. Each day he had been taken downstairs and questioned while tied to a chair. They had used their fists, Joey's own belt and even a length of classic rubber hose.

"The thing is," Joey explained. "I couldn't talk if I wanted to. They kept asking me stuff I didn't know, and I kept telling them I didn't know."

"What kinds of questions did they ask, Joey?" asked Cochran.

Joey frowned in concentration. "Well, most of the time they wanted to know things like, did I know who took Mister Zager's wallet, which I did." He looked at me. "You took his wallet, Kid, and I told them that. I'm not in trouble here, am I?"

Lynn put her hand on Joey's arm. "Don't worry, Joey. We believe you. It's just that Agent Cochran here …"

Joey's eyes widened, and he started to get up. "Agent? Nobody told me anything about feds getting involved." He glared at me. "I trusted you, Kid."

It was my turn to try. "Like Lynn said, Joey. Don't worry. You trust her, don't you?"

Joey nodded.

I continued. "Agent Cochran here is trying to figure out who killed Zager and why. He's not after you."

"You promise?"

Cochran nodded and then crossed his heart. "I promise."

That seemed to satisfy Joey, and he went back to his food.

"I thought you said they brought you food?" I said as he finished his second bowl of chili.

"Only two times a day, remember?" countered Joey with a logic I couldn't fault.

"What else did they ask you?" asked Lynn. "Why did they beat you?"

"I guess they didn't believe me. They wanted to know if I was working with The Kid and if he was working for someone else." He put a hand to his shoulder and rubbed it. "They worked me over pretty hard, but nothing they asked made any sense to me, and I told them that. I guess they finally believed me."

Earlier this evening they had tied Joey's hands, put him back in the car and headed back to the city. Joey grinned. "But I fooled them."

"Each day I pretended to be weaker than I was so that by tonight they had to drag me to the car. They did a piss-poor job of tying my wrists, giving me too much slack." He held up his hands, and we saw the angry welts and bloody abrasions. Barbara went to the sink and brought back a fresh wet washcloth.

"I knew what they planned to do. It's the look they get in their eyes and the way they don't look at your face. They were going to get rid of me." He went on to tell of the drive into the city and to the dock area. Joey had waited until the car was moving slowly between the wharves before making his move.

"There was one guy driving and one guy in the back seat with me. I pulled up my legs and jammed them into the guy next to me as hard as I could." He took another pull from the bottle, finishing it. "I think I broke a few of his ribs 'cause I heard him wheezing."

Then he threw his bound hands over the driver and got him by the throat. The driver lost control of the car and it crashed into the brick wall of a dock building.

"The airbags popped out and that stopped the driver from doing anything long enough for me to get out of the car and start running. I think I heard the driver running after me, so maybe I didn't choke him as hard as I thought, but I was far enough away that I lost him." After that Joey had taken back alleys and side streets to The Book Nook.

"You and Lynn told me you would help me." He gave a lopsided grin. "I guess I need help."

I thought about it. "What do you think, Cochran?"

Cochran nodded. "Let's keep him here for now." He turned to Lynn. "If that's okay?"

Lynn looked up at the ceiling as if visualizing the rooms above. "I think that pretty much fills the place, doesn't it, Barbara?"

Barbara laughed. "Oh, no. This is nothing. We used to put four or five to a room back in the old days of the protest marches. Of course, people have to be willing to share rooms."

A quick glance at the faces of Max, Cochran and Joey told me the answer to that question.

"I think we'll put out the No Vacancy sign," I said.

Junior chose that moment to emerge from wherever he had hidden himself when Joey arrived. He took a minute to take inventory of who was present, then hopped into Max's lap.

With his wrists and knuckles cleaned and bandaged, Joey accepted another large piece of cornbread while the rest of us tried to make sense of his story, but all we could agree upon was that the situation had just become more complicated.

Once he'd had his fill of food, I made Joey comfortable on a cot upstairs in the room where I had been practicing with the dressmaker's dummy, then headed back down to the store.

Max found me there a few minutes later.

"Son, I understand Lynn told you that this Dom DeMarco fellow and I have made our peace."

I glared at him. "Yeah, a couple of days ago from what I understand."

Max put his hand on my shoulder. "The thing is, Kid—you still don't mind if I call you that, do you? Everyone else seems to."

I sighed. "No, that's okay."

Max smiled. "Thanks. The thing is, Kid, I'm really enjoying myself. I haven't had such a good time in a coon's age. I've been on this book tour for months, putting up at hotels made out of glass and all looking the same from one city to another."

He paused and swept his hand around, encompassing all of The Book Nook. "Here I get some great home-cooked food, good company and an adventure to boot." He lowered his hand and his voice. "How about it, Kid? Mind if I stay just a few more days? I got to be in Chicago the beginning of next week."

Lynn and Barbara were right. Max did have a certain charm once you got to know him. I gave in. In return he gave me one of his slaps on the shoulder and, as usual, didn't notice me wince.

"That's great, son. Now, how's about you, me and that Cochran fellow grab a few bottles of brew and I'll tell you about the time Norman Mailer and I got into a fistfight at the National Book Awards."

Forty-Two

Our confident predictions about Doris Whitaker backing off once my cover was blown made sense, were rational, and were based both on logic and our combined knowledge of human behavior. It's too bad Doris didn't think the same way. She made her thoughts on the subject known to us the next evening.

It was a welcome quiet evening at The Book Nook. Cochran was out, hobnobbing with his fellow agents. Barbara had already retired to her room. Lynn looked in on her and reported that Barbara was lying in bed with her laptop on, well, her lap.

"I think she's looking up old schoolmates and friends from when she was young," Lynn told me as we washed and dried the dishes from dinner. "In the past few days she's asked me to help her learn to use all kinds of reunion and social web sites."

Joey was up in his room where he had stayed, except for occasional trips down the hall to use the bathroom. I'd brought him a plate of two lamb chops and couscous and a couple of cold bottles of beer earlier, but I could not entice him from his room.

"Lynn told me to stay here," he explained, "and I gotta do what Lynn says."

I was about to tell him that wasn't true when Lynn called up the stairs, telling me my dinner was getting cold, and I should get the heck down there.

"See?" said Joey.

I saw and went downstairs as I was told.

Max, Candy and April busied themselves at the table after supper, going through sheets of paper and consulting a map of the country. I listened to their conversation as I dried the dishes. An oversized road atlas was open on the table with bookmarks sticking out from many pages. "I know a fantastic old hotel in downtown Atlanta," Candy was saying. "It's central to everything and only a few blocks from the light rail."

"What about New Orleans?" asked April. "We need to schedule that after Atlanta."

Max began telling a story about New Orleans. I tuned out the conversation and put the last plate away. Max told great stories, but I had work to take care of in the store. Lynn poured herself some tea and took it over to the table and sat with the others as I left. With Lynn at the table, Max looked like an old tomcat surrounded by his ladies.

The store was quiet as befit the hour. Our only customer, a regular, bought a couple of used Dick Francis mysteries and left. Junior prowled around an old set of *The Encyclopedia Britannica*, circa 1927, rubbing his whiskers against the edges of the heavy volumes.

The bell over the door jingled as someone came into the store. I had my back to the door, scanning the shelves behind the counter for a roll of price stickers I knew I had stashed someplace last week but could not find. I wasn't being rude. Most bookstore customers like to browse a bit before coming to the counter, but this was not a customer.

"Mrs. Whitaker doesn't like you, Kid."

I wheeled around. It was Jeremy. He was wearing a V-neck sweater and slacks. With his conservative haircut he would look right at home at a country club dinner except for the gun he had pointed at me. I swallowed hard.

I tried to look around without showing the panic I was feeling. The counter would offer scant protection, as it was open at both ends. I had a moment of fleeting hope when I saw how small the gun was in his hand. I'm no expert on guns, far from it, but even my untrained eye told me it was a tiny automatic. Unfortunately, my own experience with a gun of that size forced me to recognize it was still quite lethal. I tried to stall for time.

"Let's see," I said. "You're Chad, right?"

The young man sneered. "No, I'm Jeremy. Chad's lying in bed with a cracked skull." He licked his lips, then raised the gun and pointed it at my face. "He told me to tell you goodbye."

I tried to think of another question but came up short. I saw Jeremy's fingers tighten on the little pistol. In his eyes I could see fear that matched my own.

"What the hell do you think you're doing, son?" Max's voice boomed from the back room doorway as he pushed through the hanging beads. "Don't you know those things are dangerous when they go off?"

Max walked right at Jeremy, who turned to aim at him instead of me.

I looked for something to throw at Jeremy or to hit him with, but the only objects of any size on the counter were a few heavy paperback books. I stared longingly at the stack of Max's heavy hardcover books in the center of the store.

But Max had something with which to hit Jeremy. He brought his fancy walking stick down across Jeremy's wrist with a crack. I heard the gun go off, and it fell to the floor. Jeremy, sobbing with pain and clutching his wrist, ran from the store. The front door banged against the outside wall with the force of his escape. Something touched my foot. It was Junior, taking shelter behind the counter. Relief swept through me.

Max had a foolish grin on his face. I tried to thank him for saving my life as Lynn, Candy and April came tumbling out from the back, asking what had happened.

I gave a quick rundown.

"Do you think we should call the police?" asked Lynn as she put her arm around me.

Max looked to be in shock at what had happened, as he had yet to move from where he stood. April and Candy were on either side of him, looking up at him with undisguised admiration.

"I don't think we need to." I said.

"No," said Max in a surprisingly mild voice. "No need for the police, but a doctor might be in order," and with those words his legs slowly buckled, and he sagged to the floor.

"Oh, my God. He's been shot!" said Candy and pointed to the stream of blood that was leaking at an alarming rate from his pant leg. Lynn took her cell phone from her back pocket and called 911 while the rest of us clustered around Max.

I went over to the armchairs and brought back two throw pillows. April took them and put them under Max's head. Candy sat cross-legged at the other end of the supine Max and placed the foot of his injured leg in her lap.

"We have to keep it elevated," she said to no one in particular.

I tore his pants leg away from the wound. My fingers became wet with Max's blood. I started to wipe them on my own pants and then used Max's. What the heck, they were already ruined.

The wound was mid-thigh in Max's left leg. Although the blood had soaked his pants leg, there weren't any arterial spouts of blood, and I took that as a good sign.

Lynn reached the emergency operator, knelt next to Max and described the wound.

"Get a dish towel from the kitchen," she instructed me. "We need to hold it against the wound and keep pressure on it."

I hurried into the back room. Joey was coming down the stairs.

"What's all the commotion?" he asked.

I told him what had happened while I fetched a dishtowel from the sink. It was the one I had used to dry the dishes not so many minutes ago. Joey went with me back out into the store.

Lynn took the towel, folded it and held it tightly against Max's leg.

"Hey, Kid."

Max had a goofy grin on his face. "Remind me never to do something like that again."

I told him I would, should the occasion arise.

Junior peeked his head out from behind the sales counter and walked over to Max when he saw him lying on the floor. Max scratched him behind the ears.

Lynn put hand on Joey's arm. "The police are going to be here in a few minutes."

He seemed reluctant to leave.

"Go ahead, son," Max said to him. "I got three pretty ladies taking care of me. I'll be fine." About that time we saw red and blue lights outside.

"Okay," said Joey as he edged back through the beaded curtain, "but I'll be upstairs if you need help." Joey was clearly someone who didn't like being left out of the action.

Said action increased tenfold in the next five minutes. Police and an ambulance crew swarmed into The Book Nook at the same time. For a moment I thought a fight was going to break out between the two teams as each tried to show they were in charge.

"Boys! Hey! Let's focus, shall we?" called Max in a voice more powerful than I thought he could manage, given the circumstances. Evidently it took quite a bit out of him, as his face paled, and he laid his head back on the small pillow.

His shout did the trick, though, and soon he was on a stretcher being carried from the store with all of us following. I worried there would be some contention between Candy and April as to who would ride in the ambulance with Max, but that was solved before it started. Both Candy and April climbed into the back with the stretcher.

The door closed seconds later, and the ambulance took off. Its siren sounded long after it disappeared around the corner and headed down Oak Street to Mercy hospital. Only minutes after it all began, Lynn and I found we were standing by ourselves on the dark street outside the bookstore.

Back inside the store we found two uniformed police officers trying to make sense of what had happened. I'm afraid I didn't help much with the scant answers I gave. I wasn't certain just how much I could say. I certainly couldn't tell them that a rival pickpocket had shot Max.

Fortunately, Cochran showed up and flashed his FBI badge. That got their attention. One of them went outside and spoke into his radio for a minute, then came back inside.

"We're supposed to just hang tight until Sergeant Green arrives."

I was disappointed that Mel wouldn't be taking charge of the mess. Barbara joined us about that time, resplendent in a woolen bathrobe of patchwork colors. Her hair was down from her braids, and she looked like I'd always imagined Eleanor, the Dowager Queen, would look.

She offered the two policemen some tea, but they declined.

"Some coffee perhaps? I expect you work fairly late into the night." If it weren't for the mischievous sparkle in her eye, I would have bought the part she was playing for them.

They had no problem buying her act, though. "No thank you, Ma'am," said the one who had radioed in and appeared to be senior to his fellow. "Perhaps you and the others would like to wait somewhere?"

Barbara smiled. "No, thank you," she answered. She walked over to one of the easy chairs and sat down, pulling her feet up under her. "I'm quite comfortable."

Lynn took the chair next to Barbara and sat in a similar fashion. She gave me a sly smile.

"You know, Kid. Some tea would be nice. Why don't you fetch some for Barbara and me, please?"

I sighed. Joey was right, no denying it. I turned to Cochran. "Do you want tea, too?"

He shook his head with a smile.

I went out into the kitchen and began filling the ancient water kettle. Someone gets shot in my store, police are everywhere, an FBI agent is underfoot, and what do I do? I put the kettle on for tea.

Forty-Three

When Sgt. Green showed up, his name clicked into place. Evidently he recognized Cochran and me, as well. His toothpick moved from one side of his mouth to the other as he regarded us.

"You two again? I remember you from last year." He studied Cochran's identity card for a second and handed it back, then turned to me. "You a fed, too?"

I explained that Lynn and I owned the store.

"Whatever. So what's the story you're going to tell me?"

I proceeded to tell him how someone had tried to hold up the store and how Max had come to my rescue. I pointed to Jeremy's little automatic on the floor where he had dropped it.

"We haven't touched the gun."

The toothpick switched sides again. "Gee, thanks." He told one of the cops to put the gun in an evidence bag. He told the other to find the ejected shell. We all watched in silence as the officer shined his flashlight around the floor until its brass casing glowed back in response.

"Got it," he said as he dropped it into a small plastic bag.

Sgt. Green accepted both the gun and the shell and sent the uniformed cops on their way. He spent a few more minutes asking routine questions, then worked his toothpick and said goodbye. He turned back as he opened door.

"I'll visit your friend at the hospital in the morning. If you do think of anything you'd like to share with a lowly sergeant, let me know, won't you?"

Cochran and I promised we would, but he gave no sign he heard us as he left.

Once he was gone we all trooped to the back room, where we gathered as usual around the table.

"So what really happened?" asked Cochran.

I let Lynn tell the story.

"Well," said Cochran after she was done, "it looks as if Doris Whitaker is still after you, Kid. That's not good." A wry smile came to his face. "It's not like my staying here did much good to keep her crew away. Short of shutting down the store and Lynn's studio, I don't know what else to suggest."

"We could close up for a few weeks," I suggested. "Maybe all this will blow over by then."

Barbara's teacup clattered on its saucer as she put it down.

"Kid!" she said sharply. "I'm surprised at you."

We all looked at her. Even in the dim light of the kitchen her eyes were bright.

"This store has been open since the sixties. We were here through the civil rights marches and the riots after dear Doctor King's assassination. We were proudly in the middle of the anti-war movement and protests. Women's rights, gay rights, there isn't a righteous cause we weren't part of." She lowered her voice. "And I'll be damned if I see this store close because of a cheap hoodlum like Doris Whitaker."

Barbara peered at Cochran. "What's keeping you from locking her up for good? Personally, I'm tired of that woman. I didn't like her half a century ago when she was working badger games, and I certainly don't like her now. Lock her up, why don't you?"

Cochran struggled for an answer. "It's not that easy, Barbara. The DA will need a good witness, someone who has personally dealt with her and would be willing to testify against her. She's done too good a job of protecting herself with her crew."

An idea came to me. "Cochran," I said. "I think I know just the person they need."

"You do?"

"Could you get him into the witness protection program?"

Cochran nodded. "It's possible, if his testimony is good enough."

"Could he pick where he's relocated to?"

"Within reason."

I smiled. This just might work.

Forty-Four

After breakfast the next morning Cochran and I headed out. I took him down to City Center, where we bought coffee from a sidewalk vendor and watched the mid-morning crowd. I kept looking and watching until I found the guy I wanted. As instructed, Cochran hung back, following me at a distance as I approached our man.

Jay glanced up as my shadow reached him. He was perched on a low wall of white cement near the center of the plaza. His normally cheerful face showed concern when he recognized me, and he looked around nervously.

"Hey, Kid," he said quietly as I sat next to him. "I hear Doris is on the warpath for you. I warned you about her. It's like she's gone crazy."

"Yeah, she sent one of her boys to my bookshop last night."

Jay's eyebrows went up.

"He took a shot at me but got a friend of mine instead." I looked Jay in the eye. "Now I'm on the warpath, if you get my meaning."

Jay started to get up. I stuck my arm out and held him in place. A second later Cochran joined us, sitting next to him on the other side.

Jay's eyes darted from me to Cochran and back to me again. "What's going on, Kid?" There was a note of panic in his voice. I kept my arm in place but tried to reassure him.

"Don't worry, Jay. It's nothing you won't like. In fact, this gentleman here," I nodded to Cochran, "just might be able to make your fondest wish come true."

Jay stared at me as though I was crazy.

I continued. "You remember telling me about how you and Dave want to quit the fencing business and move to Key West?"

Jay gave an uncertain nod.

"Well, then today is your lucky day."

"What? How?" Jay's voice trailed off into sputters.

"Jay," I said, "this is Agent Cochran of the FBI. Let's sit here a little while so you can hear what he has to offer you."

Jay swallowed. Cochran began talking.

It took a lot longer than I expected, as Jay's fear of Doris was enormous. But the lure of being able to start a new life with new names in Key West for him and his partner Dave was too much for him to resist.

An hour later we left the plaza. I was headed back to The Book Nook, and Jay and Cochran were headed for the federal building. An agent was already on his way to pick up Dave at their apartment. Cochran didn't want to give Doris any chance of causing trouble.

"Wait!" Jay stopped walking before they were more than a few feet away. "What about our things?"

"We'll have a team over there within an hour and pack it all up for you," Cochran assured him.

"But what about Lily?"

"Lily is Jay and Dave's dog," I explained.

"Is she very big?" Cochran asked. "Will she cause them trouble?"

Jay was offended. "Lily is the sweetest little dog in the world."

"Then don't worry. They'll bring Lily to the federal building."

"Tell them to bring a muzzle," I told Cochran in a whisper so Jay wouldn't hear me malign his dog. "Lily is small, but she's a demon."

They walked off together, and I stopped and watched them. If all went well, I'd never see Jay again. I thought about that phrase, *if all goes well.* Cochran had used it only a few minutes ago as he explained to Jay the wonderful world inside the witness protection program.

He certainly made it sound easy.

Forty-Five

There was a message on the store's answering machine when I returned. I had a pen and paper ready to take a request to find a book, but I put the pen down when I heard the precise, flat voice on the other end.

"Mr. Smith? This is Metcalf. I've got something I believe you and Agent Cochran have been looking for. It's the missing memory card. I've already called Agent Cochran. He's coming to my hotel suite. He suggested I invite you, as well, though I don't really see why."

The guy was condescending even when leaving a message. What he didn't realize was that I might not have gone had he not added that dig. My work was really beginning to stack up at the store. I put my jacket back on as Lynn came out from the back room.

"Where are you going? I thought you were going to try to get the ordering done today."

I told her of Metcalf's call and Cochran's request that I join them. Lynn disappeared into the back room for a few seconds and then returned, putting on her own coat. Seconds after that Joey followed, wearing his black leather jacket.

I put my hands on my hips. "You don't have to go."

Lynn ignored me and picked up her purse.

I looked at Joey. He started to explain, but I cut him off. "Yes, I know, where Lynn goes, you go. Okay, let's all go."

We walked the half-dozen blocks, fighting the rush hour crowds all the way. The elevator operator raised his eyebrows when he saw I had company but didn't object. He took us to the penthouse floor and let us out. "Mr. Metcalf said to let you find the door yourself." He appeared miffed at this breach of protocol.

"I know the door, thank you." I told him.

He still looked doubtful but pressed his gloved finger to a button, and the doors slid closed.

"This way," I told Lynn and Joey, and we headed down the hallway. I knocked on the door.

"Come in," called Cochran. His voice was faint. I opened the door, and we went inside. Cochran and Metcalf were nowhere in sight.

"Kid, is that you?" called Cochran. "We're out here on the patio."

The curtains to the windows were drawn, but one billowed where the open patio door was. We crossed the large living room of the suite and pushed through the curtains.

It's odd, but I could smell death before I saw the body. Perhaps it was the trace of gunpowder in the air. I saw a man's body lying near the center of the patio. He lay on his back, and bloody bullet wounds marked where he had been shot in the heart. It was Newcomb, the deadly and expensive hit man.

Metcalf sat in a chair next to a patio table about ten feet away. He rested his head on one hand. He gave us a disinterested look as we emerged onto the patio. A gun lay on the table.

Cochran was speaking on his cell phone near the sliding door. He held up a hand to forestall questions, finished his conversation and hung up. He put his cell phone back into his pocket.

"Looks like you guys came up for nothing," he said. "Any meeting will have to wait until the police arrive and clear the scene."

"What happened?" asked Lynn.

"That's Newcomb, the hit man hired by Wolfe, isn't it?" I asked.

Cochran nodded. "That's him. He's dead."

"You shot him?" I asked. "What was he doing here?"

Cochran shook his head and pointed over at Metcalf.

"No, Metcalf shot him just as I arrived. I heard the shots from outside in the hall." He glanced over at Metcalf and lowered his voice. "He says Newcomb arrived about half an hour ago, right after he called to let me know he had the memory card. He was outside on the patio when Newcomb came out there. He doesn't know how Newcomb got into the suite, but you and I know it isn't that difficult if you're a professional."

I didn't like being lumped in with a professional killer but couldn't argue the point.

Cochran continued. "To tell the truth, I don't know if Newcomb was here to kill Metcalf or not. I kind of doubt it. But Metcalf had a gun in the pocket of that robe he's wearing. That's it on the table next to him. He figured Wolfe had decided to get rid of him, and he shot Newcomb without waiting to see if it was true."

Metcalf must have been listening, as he spoke up when Cochran finished telling us what had happened. His voice was a hollow echo of its former self.

"I've never seen anyone die before like that, let alone kill someone. It's like it was someone else pulling the trigger. I can't believe I did it." He raised his head. "I know it's rude, but could someone bring me a drink? There's some brandy in the bar inside."

Metcalf was one of those people who expect others to do as they ask, and Joey was one of those who do it. "I'll get it," he said and brushed back the curtains and went into the suite's living room.

I marveled at Joey's willingness to follow orders and at Metcalf's ability to give them. As I did, a flash of clarity hit me. In the space of a moment the events of the past week clicked into place, and I saw the whole sorry story unfold in my mind.

"And the data card," I asked, "where is that?"

My question took Cochran by surprise. "Kid, given the circumstances, I think that can wait, don't you?"

I shook my head. "No, Cochran, I don't think it can."

Lynn and Cochran stared at me. Behind me in the living room, Joey clattered glasses and bottles.

The patio was as it had been the other day with the afternoon sun streaming from behind tall surrounding buildings, traffic sounds rising from the street and birds overhead. It was as though everything had stopped. I took a breath and plunged in.

"So where is it?" I asked Metcalf in a loud voice. "Where's the data card?"

He reached into an inside pocket and brought out a tiny square of plastic. He held it up for us to see.

"Here it is, Mr. Smith. Satisfied?"

I turned to face Cochran. "How about it, Cochran? It that the data card that is chock full of data and details about Wolfe's operation? Enough information to put him away for good?"

"That's what it's supposed to contain. We'll have to dump its contents back at the office and then consult with the finance and legal experts. It'll probably take days or weeks to fully understand how Wolfe's operations work."

"Yeah, right," I answered. "In the meantime Metcalf, here, gets full immunity from prosecution for any and all crimes he may have committed."

Metcalf, finally showing interest in our conversation, got to his feet.

Cochran spread his hands. "That's the way it works, Kid. He's giving us the information we need to extradite Wolfe and shut down his operations. That card and his testimony will make the indictments ironclad. Talbot may have died trying to get there, but we are going to make certain Wolfe goes down."

I shook my head. "Cochran, don't you realize that Metcalf was only playing Talbot? Just like he's playing you now?"

Joey chose that moment to emerge from the room, carrying a tumbler with amber liquid.

A thin voice cut through the air. "Very good, Mr. Smith."

Metcalf stood facing us, holding a pistol. He pointed it at Cochran. "Please, Agent Cochran, don't make any sudden movements." He licked his lips. "I have to give this some thought."

Cochran stood stock still with his arms at his side. Lynn stepped close to me and took hold of my arm. Joey put the drink down on a small table near the door.

There weren't too many ways this could turn out, and pretty much all of them were bad. The pistol he had used to kill Newcomb was tantalizingly close to us. Maybe Cochran could make use of it if he had a chance. I made an effort at distracting Metcalf.

"Since your pistol is on the table, I'm assuming that's Newcomb's gun. You took it and put it into your pocket before you let Cochran in." Metcalf nodded, obviously not much distracted.

I continued. "Newcomb didn't come here to kill you. He came here to report to you, didn't he?"

Metcalf smiled. "Why would he do that, Mister Smith?"

"Because he's been working for you all along. You're the one who hired him to kill the currier and to kill Talbot."

Cochran started to object, but I continued my explanation before he could speak. "Metcalf needed to kill Zager because he was the only one who knew that Wolfe never gave him the memory card to begin with. There never was a memory card filled with information. That card he showed us is just a dummy. It's probably got stuff on it but nothing of any value, right?"

"Very good, Mr. Smith, very good," said Metcalf. "Do go on."

I did. "Don't you see, Cochran? This whole thing was nothing but a scam by Metcalf to obtain immunity. He had no intention of giving evidence against Wolfe."

A second flash of inspiration hit me. I turned back to Metcalf. "John Wolfe is dead, isn't he? You've been running his operation."

"What are you talking about?" Cochran asked.

I looked at the lawyer. "Do you want to tell him, or should I?"

An annoyed look crossed his face. "I suppose I should. Mr. Smith is correct, Agent Cochran. John Wolfe died over a year ago. No," he said. "I didn't kill him, though in hindsight I could have. He died of a heart attack. I was there when it happened. I was the only one there, and I realized that he was even more useful to me dead than alive. That's when I contacted Talbot about providing evidence in return for immunity and protection."

"Protection from a dead man," Lynn said.

"That's right, my dear. And now I'm afraid it's time to bring this little charade to an end."

Joey spoke up from behind me. "You mean you hired the bastard who killed the guy I was supposed to be protecting?"

A peeved look came to Metcalf's face. "Does it really matter? I'll just need to rearrange the story a little. Newcomb here," he nodded toward the body of the hit man, "shot and killed the four of you, I heard the shots, came out on the patio and shot him."

Lynn held my arm tighter.

Cochran spoke. "You don't have to do it this way."

Metcalf shook his head. "Sorry, Agent Cochran. The only question now is who goes first."

There was a growl behind me. "You gonna shoot Lynn?"

Joey pushed past me. With one movement he swept up the bag of golf clubs and held it front of him in both hands. He walked fast, almost at a run, toward Metcalf.

Metcalf raised the gun and shot twice, and then twice again. At least one shot went wide and a window shattered behind us. I think a couple of shots hit the bag and at least one shot hit Joey, as I saw him falter in his run. Metcalf stepped backward and kept shooting as he did, but Joey closed the gap between them quickly.

Then, before what was happening could really register with us, Joey and Metcalf were at the parapet at the building's edge. There was no way Metcalf missed Joey with his next shot, but Joey's momentum keep him moving, and with the bag of golf clubs like a battering ram, he ran into Metcalf. For a moment they teetered on the edge, and then Metcalf, the bag of golf clubs and Joey went over the side.

The three of us ran to where they went over and looked down. Twelve stories down, two figures lay on the street. Cars were stopping, and we could hear shouts and screams. By some small miracle, as far as I could tell, no one on the street below had been injured. Several people looked up at where we were and pointed.

"Oh, my God, Kid," cried Lynn. "Poor Joey."

Cochran took out his cell phone and called his office.

Lynn and I turned away from the sight below and hugged each other. I looked around at the patio. It still resembled something out of a decorator magazine with its designer patio furniture, potted plants and trees and putting green. It was picture-perfect except for Newcomb's body and two golf clubs lying where they'd fallen from the bag as Joey rushed Metcalf.

Cochran put down his cell phone. "The police will be here in a few minutes. I'm going inside to let them in when they arrive." He looked at Lynn and me. "You know the drill."

I nodded. "Don't touch anything," I said.

He gave a rueful smile and left.

Forty-Six

Just when we thought it was over, it wasn't.

Three days had passed since Joey died saving us. Max was back from the hospital to spend one last night at The Book Nook before heading out to Chicago. I wondered how Candy was going to take that. She and April had remained by his hospital bedside for most of his stay there.

It was mid-afternoon, and the store was quiet with only a couple of customers browsing through the shelves. I was sitting on the floor, unpacking a box of books.

Cochran walked in, and he wasn't alone. Special Agents Cranz and Stern were with him. The look on their faces as they came into the store gave me a sinking feeling in my stomach.

"Hi, Kid," said Cochran. There was trouble in his eyes. "You already know Agents Cranz and Stern."

I nodded. This obviously wasn't a social call.

"Is Barbara here?"

I nodded again. "Yes, she's in the back room. Go on back. I'll be there in a second." I glanced over at Old Tom.

He waved from his place behind the counter.

Cochran led the other two agents into the back room.

I stood up and surveyed the store as if for the last time. One of the browsing customers had left, leaving only one man. He was an older black man, tall and wearing a dashiki. He might have been out of place at another bookstore, but here he looked at home.

I really loved The Book Nook. It had been the one constant, the one place of refuge for me that I could count on as I grew up. Lynn and I had put everything we had into it. Then there was

Barbara. The store held Barbara's soul. I couldn't imagine her not living here just as I couldn't imagine The Book Nook not existing.

I breathed in a lungful of air, tasting the tang of old books, wood shelves and time, and then I headed for the back room.

Forty-Seven

Barbara, Lynn and Cochran sat at the table. Agents Cranz and Stern stood behind Cochran, who looked up at me as I pushed through the beaded curtains and then continued with what he was saying. He held a piece of paper folded lengthwise. It looked familiar.

"I'm sorry, Barbara, but the bureau can't ignore this warrant and the reason it was issued. If this warrant didn't exist, there wouldn't be a problem. None of us want to do this."

Stern and Cranz nodded in agreement. Cochran handed the warrant to Agent Cranz, who put it in his coat pocket.

"But the warrant exists, and these agents have to take you into custody." Cochran looked at me. "The store will have to be regarded as ill-gotten gains until and unless Barbara can show otherwise."

"I don't care about the store," I said, "but we had a deal." I could feel my face getting red. "I went along with what Talbot wanted. He said he wouldn't go after Barbara if I did what he wanted, and I kept my side of the bargain."

"But Agent Talbot is dead, and we can find nothing to confirm that," Agent Stern replied.

"This is so unfair," said Lynn. "We trusted Talbot, and we trusted you, Cochran."

Cochran could only look down at the table while I looked at Barbara. To my surprise she smiled, and lifted her shoulders. "Life is certainly a long, strange journey, isn't it, Kid?"

I couldn't believe she was taking this so lightly. "Barbara, don't you understand? There will be a trial that could drag on for over a year. We'll lose the bookstore, and you could end up in jail."

"Now don't get upset." Barbara reached up and took my hand. "You know things always work out for the best. Besides, I've heard that jail food has gotten a lot better since the last time I was there."

I looked at Lynn to see if she could get through to Barbara about how serious things were. A movement behind us caused the beaded curtain to click. I turned. The older man I had seen in the bookstore had come in.

"Sir," said Agent Cranz. "I'll have to ask you to leave."

The man ignored him. "Hello, Barbara," he said softly. His voice was a deep baritone with shades of an accent.

Barbara studied his face for a few seconds, and then her eyes lit up. "Jimmie? Jimmie LeCuyer?"

The man nodded. "I got word you were in trouble, something to do with a little bank robbery a few years ago?"

Barbara jumped to her feet and went to him. She took both of his hands in hers and gazed up into his face. "Oh, it's so good to see you," she said. "You didn't mind coming?"

"No," he answered with a tender tone. "I knew it was time."

Cochran pushed back his chair and got to his feet. He faced LeCuyer.

"Mister James LeCuyer?" he asked in a formal voice.

LeCuyer answered in kind. "I am, sir, and you are?"

Cochran brought out his identity card and opened it. "Agent Cochran of the FBI. It is my duty to arrest you in connection with the robbery of the First Federal Bank of Madison, Wisconsin, and the death of the bank guard." Cochran went on to recite the familiar Miranda rights statement. He ended with, "Do you understand these rights as I have presented them?"

LeCuyer, still holding Barbara's hands, nodded.

"I do," he said, "but before we leave I'd like to say something in front of witnesses."

Cochran signaled his agreement, and LeCuyer continued. "I'd like to say for the record that after the bombing and during the week I stayed here, Barbara Jenkins had no idea I was a wanted man, nor did she receive any of the money I may or may not have stolen from that bank." He stared at Cochran. "I will so testify in any statement I make and at any trial that is held." He held Cochran's gaze. "Do we understand each other?"

Cochran looked at Cranz and Stern. They nodded. He turned back to LeCuyer. "Yes, sir, I believe we do." Suddenly he stuck out his hand. LeCuyer appeared startled for a moment, and then he released one of his hands from Barbara's and shook hands with Cochran.

I caught Lynn's eye, and we both smiled. There was a reason we liked Cochran.

Agents Cranz and Stern left the store with Jimmy LeCuyer in custody. Cochran went with them as far as the front of the store. If it weren't such a serious situation, it would have been comical as we watched the two beefy agents, Cochran and LeCuyer try to get through the beaded curtain at the same time.

Barbara was cheerful as she called goodbye to LeCuyer and promised to visit him as soon as he was booked and in jail, but as she went to the stove and put the kettle on for tea, I spotted the glint of tears in her eyes.

Cochran returned and took his seat again at the table.

We drank our tea in silence, all of us stunned by what had happened. Finally Lynn spoke up.

"Those errands you've been running, Barbara? And all that searching on line? You were trying to get word to James LeCuyer, weren't you?"

Barbara nodded. "I was hoping he would give a deposition from wherever he was, clearing me of any involvement in the bank robbery." She shook her head. "I never dreamed that he would come back in person."

An unpleasant thought came to my mind. "Cochran, as long as that arrest warrant exists, this could come up again. Isn't there any way we can file some kind of motion to have it rescinded?"

Cochran leaned back in his chair, a slight smile on his face. "I have an idea that that arrest warrant is never going to be seen again."

"What do you mean?"

Cochran reached under his left shirt cuff and removed a piece of paper. It was folded lengthwise and looked very familiar. He tossed it on the table. The rest of us simply stared. Cochran's smile grew wider.

It finally dawned on me. "You took the warrant from Cranz's pocket when you were crowding through the door with them, didn't you?"

Cochran's smile was as wide as it could get. "Actually, it was Stern who had it, but yes. So tell me, did I pass the test?"

I laughed and clapped him on the shoulder.

"But," asked Lynn, "those are all computerized. Can't they simply print another?"

Cochran shook his head. "They would have to ask the judge to sign it again, and with James LeCuyer's statement exonerating Barbara, there's not much chance of that."

Our uproarious laughter filled the back room of The Book Nook. The sound of it brought Old Tom from the front of the store to see what the commotion was. He stared at the sight of a saucepan on the table with a burning piece of paper in it.

Tom adjusted his wireframe glasses. "I suppose there's a rational reason behind all this?"

"Absolutely," I answered, straight faced. "We are celebrating Agent Cochran's graduation from Pickpocket University."

Forty-Eight

Dinner was a bittersweet affair that night. Max stumped into the back room, leaning on his walking stick, with Candy on one arm and April on the other. He accepted my offer of a chair and lowered himself into it, wincing a little as he did.

"It's a real shame about that Joey fellow," he said, "but he saved your lives, and we shall hoist a brew in his honor."

I got the hint and fetched a bottle of beer from the refrigerator and a glass from the cupboard and put them on the table in front of him.

"Thanks, Kid," he said, opening the bottle and pouring beer into the glass. He waited for the foam to subside and then lifted the glass. "Here's to Joey, a good man." He took a long pull from the glass. Duty done, he set the glass down. He leaned back in his chair and let his eyes wander around the kitchen. "I'm going to miss this place, Kid. I hope you don't mind if I stop in again the next time I'm in the area."

I told him that was fine, and I meant it. Max had his rough edges, but I'd grown to enjoy his company.

"The fact is I'm already planning my next book. It's going to be set in Monterey in 1948, and it is going to tell the true story of what happened to Doc Ricketts. I'm kind of thinking that it might involve a pickpocket, so I may need to consult you, if you don't mind."

I assured Max I'd be available for such a consultation.

Junior strolled into the back room a few minutes later, and Max scooped him up. "I'm going to miss you, too, you handsome devil," he said as he scratched the top of Junior's head. Junior closed his eyes and purred in reply.

April Quist spoke up. "I've got an announcement of my own."

We turned our attention to her.

She looked down at the table, gathered her courage and raised her eyes to us. "I'm quitting my job as event coordinator for Max," she said. "I'm going to write a book, too."

"And it's about damn time," said Max. "Haven't I been telling you that you're wasting your time trying to keep an old goat like me on schedule?"

"What's the book about?" I asked.

April laughed. "Ask Lynn."

"April, with help from Candy and me, has gotten a job as a dancer at The Pink Poodle," Lynn said with a smile. "Her book is going to be about the life of a stripper. I'm helping her learn the routines. I think she'll do fine, and I also think it's about time someone wrote about all the stuff women like Candy and me have had to go through."

April grinned. "Max's editor has already agreed to look at the book when it's ready."

Everyone at the table applauded.

"Max, how are you going to replace her?" I asked.

"Already taken care of," he said, looking over his shoulder at Candy. "Miss Candy here has agreed to take on that job. It turns out she's got contacts all over the country."

Candy nodded. "That's right," she said. "I figure it's long past time for me to make use of a life spent on the road. Besides, someone's got to keep an eye on Max."

"That's not the only job she's taking on," said Max. He reached up over his shoulder and took Candy's hand. "You tell them, Doll."

Candy blushed. "Max and I are getting married."

Naturally, that was cause for more bottles to be opened, drinks poured and toasts made. April got out her camera and took pictures. One of my favorite photographs to this day is from that evening. It shows Max sitting at the table with Candy on his lap and Junior on her lap. She has one arm around Max's shoulders. Barbara is standing to one side, and Lynn and I are on the other, and we are all holding our glasses up as a toast is made. Someone, probably Max, had just told a joke, and our faces are lit with laughter and love.

Forty-Nine

Cochran called my cell phone at ten o'clock the next morning.

"Hi, Kid. Can you, Barbara and Lynn meet me for coffee in an hour? I guarantee it will be worth your time for all three of you."

I doubted the others would agree. I certainly wasn't interested in budging from the store. We were all pretty wiped out by the events of the past few days.

We were in the kitchen. I put my hand over the phone and told Lynn and Barbara what he wanted.

"Where?" ask Lynn, ever the practical one.

I asked him. It was one of those chain coffee shops that have become ubiquitous throughout the country. Lynn and Barbara shook their heads, but Cochran was insistent, and we gave in.

We made a quick check to see that we were reasonably presentable and piled into Lynn's car. Barbara let me sit up front with Lynn. It was almost like a luxury for me.

We parked on a side street, and a minute later we arrived at the coffee shop.

"Look," said Barbara, pointing into the shop's front window. "There's Agent Cochran. He's waving to us." She waved back at Cochran.

Lynn and I didn't pay attention. Our eyes were focused on the building across the street. I had thought the address of the coffee shop sounded familiar. Now I knew why.

The coffee shop was directly across the street from The Empire Room. In a flash I had an idea why Cochran wanted us there. I stole a glance at Lynn. The brightness of her smile told me she had figured it out, as well.

We went inside and joined Cochran at the counter.

"My treat," he said. Barbara ordered Chamomile tea. Lynn asked for a cappuccino. I decided to go all out and ordered what I call a candy-bar-in-a-cup. That's one of those crushed ice and coffee drinks with caramel swirled in. Lynn heard me order it and patted my stomach. I ignored her. Cochran ordered a simple black coffee.

It took a few minutes for us to receive our drinks with mine taking the longest. Cochran kept looking at his watch and out the front door. As soon as I had my drink, he hustled us out the door and onto the sidewalk.

"Now what?" I asked as I sipped my drink.

Cochran grinned and pointed down the street. As if on cue, a large black SUV and a city police car came into view. They drove fast and seconds later screeched to a stop in front of The Empire Room. A second police car arrived from the other direction. Traffic on the street came to a stop, and a small crowd formed quickly with everyone, like us, watching the show.

Four people in suits, two women and two men, climbed out of the SUV. One of them was talking on a cell phone. They were joined by uniformed police officers, six of them, from the patrol cars. They huddled for a minute and then streamed up the steps and into The Empire Room.

I thought about how Lynn and I had run down those steps only days before, Lynn carrying her spiked heels and wearing that silly outfit with her blonde wig falling off. I think Lynn sensed what I was thinking, because when I gave her a grin, she poked me. But she was smiling, too.

Several minutes ticked by. Some of the pedestrians who had stopped to watch the action gave up and left, but word must have gotten out on the street that something was happening, as the crowd continued to grow. I recognized several pickpockets who'd run afoul of Doris, as well as a fence or two, plus a handful of panhandlers, street preachers and others who live on the margin of society. Even Molly Munn showed up with her cart. A pair of traffic cops routed cars around the stopped police cars and the FBI's SUV.

The four of us kept our eyes on the doors of The Empire Room and sipped our drinks. We didn't mind waiting. A paddy wagon drove up the street and parked directly in front. A jail warden got out of the passenger seat and opened the doors in the back.

At last the doors to The Empire Room swung open. The first to emerge were three of Doris's crew. I saw Jeremy and Chad among them. Their hands were handcuffed in front of them. Jeremy was easy to spot by the cast on his wrist and Chad by the bandage on his head. They were led by uniformed officers and put into the paddy wagon. Lynn took my hand, and I squeezed hers in return.

Finally the big moment came. Doris Whitaker was brought out of The Empire Room and down the broad steps. A small crowd of well-dressed men and women followed behind her, diners in The Empire Room who had been startled and confused by the forcible removal of one of their most revered fellow diners. Several tagged along with Doris's escorts, obviously protesting their actions. People in the crowd began holding up their cell phones and snapping pictures.

Someone in the crowd called out her name. "Hey, Doris! Look over here."

Someone else called, "Hey, Doris, smile for the camera!"

The two women FBI agents and two policewomen escorted her down the stairs. Her wrists were in handcuffs, and when I saw her shuffling walk, I realized she was wearing shackles on her ankles, as well.

Doris Whitaker was a mess. Her carefully coifed hair was in disarray, the thick makeup on her face was smeared, and her fashionable dress had ridden up behind her, exposing the backs of her legs.

Her cultivated looks were not all that Doris lost that morning. She snarled at the crowd and cursed them, the police and the FBI. Then she caught sight of us across the street. Her shouts became incoherent shrieks as she called us every name in the book and then some. The crowd noticed at whom she was directing her wrath, and I began to think we should withdraw back into the coffee shop.

Before I could suggest it, Barbara stepped off the sidewalk, crossed the street and headed straight toward Doris. Barbara was a tiny woman in stature, but as she crossed the street she was like nothing less than an avenging angel.

As one, Cochran, Lynn and I started after her and caught up to her just as she reached Doris. Barbara placed herself directly in Doris's path. The policewomen and FBI agents didn't seem to know what to do with the force of nature that is Barbara when she is angry.

The watching crowd, sensing something unusual was happening, grew quiet. Barbara addressed Doris in a voice razor sharp and twice as cutting.

"Doris Whitaker, you painted hussy. You have been a blight on this city far too long. I knew you forty years ago when you were a cheap tart who shamed our sex when you hustled tricks on Broadway." Doris's face reddened. Barbara continued, listing every one of Doris's sins for all to hear and stripping her of every pretense of respectability.

The crowd around us listened in rapt attention. Her fellow customers of The Empire Room, hearing Barbara's litany of Doris's crimes, began edging away, reconsidering their show of public support. At the height of his legendary speaking skills, Daniel Webster could not have delivered a more damning speech.

"I don't know what kind of sentence you are going to receive or to what prison they will send you, Doris Whitaker," Barbara finished as her eyes flashed with anger, "but should some day in the future you be released from jail, don't you dare return to sully the air of our city again. So help me, if you do …" and here

Barbara raised her hand as if to slap her. Doris recoiled, all her pride and fight withered away under Barbara's scolding.

I stepped forward to stop her, but Barbara lowered her hand. "Don't worry, Doris," she said in a glacial voice. "I wouldn't stain my hand by touching that cheap, painted face of yours." She turned her back on Doris and walked back to where Lynn and I were standing.

Lynn began to clap, Cochran joined her, and then so did I. Others picked up the applause, and pretty soon the whole crowd was applauding, cheering Barbara and bidding good riddance to Doris.

Barbara linked her arms with Lynn and me. "Come along, you two," she said with a happy smile. "Let's go home."

I suppose Doris was put into the paddy wagon and taken off to jail. I wouldn't know. We never looked back.

Meet Author Andrew MacRae

Andrew MacRae is a misplaced Midwesterner now living in California. He works in the high tech field and is the creator of the Virtual Globe Theatre, a model of Shakespeare's theater as it stood in 1599.

He has had several mystery and crime stories published as well as slipstream, historical stories and children's stories and poetry. His mystery novels, *Murder Misdirected* and *Murder Miscalculated,* are both published by Mainly Murder Press.

In his spare time Andrew leads a monthly folk music jam, hosts a monthly open mike, presents showings of classic movies, produces concerts and staged radio shows and serves on an historic architecture review board.

~

For more great mysteries from fresh, new authors visit www.MainlyMurderPress.com

Sample of
Murder Misdirected

by Andrew MacRae

Prologue

A nervous man sat in an anonymous coffee shop in the center of the city, the fingers of one hand drumming on his knee. It was early afternoon, and he had hours to kill before meeting his partner. Having betrayed his employer's trust, he now understood a simple cruel truth, that trust betrayed for one is trust betrayed for all. Could he trust his partner? Did his partner trust him? The man took his hand from his knee and held it in front of him, trying to will it to cease its motion. He reached for his coffee, misjudged where it was and knocked over the paper cup. It was almost empty, and what spilled was easily wiped up with a paper napkin, yet the man saw it as a sign. He put the napkin down and looked at his hand again. It was still shaking. The man put his hand back under the table, where it found his knee, and his fingers began their drumming again.

Betrayal, too, was on another man's mind in another part of the city as he placed a thin metal case on a hotel bed and unlocked it. From the case he removed an automatic pistol and silencer. He fitted one to the other and contemplated the coming course of events. Killing his partner was not of great concern to him. It was only a logical step in the path he had taken. The man placed the assembled pistol and silencer into a shoulder holster and tightened the straps. He put on his suit coat and checked himself in the mirror to ensure the gun did not show. He looked at the clock on the table next to the bed. He had hours to kill before meeting his partner.

One

A fat, easy score, that's all I wanted, and it's what I desperately needed. What I didn't know, couldn't know, was the murderous chain of events that my need of cash was going to set into motion. I was back in town after three long months of watching Fast Eddie slowly die and finally burying him when he did. Eddie's funeral and our extended stay back east that preceded it had consumed all my money and then some. I didn't begrudge the money or the time spent, though. Eddie was my friend and my mentor, but it meant I was going to have to hustle if I wanted to avoid trouble.

The driver of the last ride I hitched wasn't going anywhere near downtown, but Lynn's apartment house wasn't much out of his way, and so he dropped me there. We shared the brief goodbyes of strangers through an open car window after I unloaded my small suitcase and garment bag, and he took off down the dark and empty street while I went inside the apartment house and climbed the stairs to the second floor.

I put my suitcase down on the scuffed linoleum in the darkened hallway in front of Lynn's door and gave a few tentative raps with my knuckles. I didn't want to disturb Lynn's neighbors, so I stood there for almost a minute before realizing she was bound to be sound asleep and politeness wouldn't work. I almost turned and left, but in the early hours of the morning and with only a few dollars in my pocket, I had nowhere else to go.

I knocked again, this time with force, and kept on knocking for a full minute. I didn't stop until I saw the doorknob turn. The door opened a couple of inches until a chain stopped it. Lynn's angular face looked sleepily out at me. She blinked until her eyes focused and she recognized me. I gestured with the hand that held my garment bag and gave her what I hoped was a sincere smile with just a trace of a woebegone child.

"Oh, God, I should have known. Who else would wake me up at four in the morning?" Lynn closed the door again and for a fraction of a second I thought she was going to leave me out in the hallway. Then I heard the chain fall loose.

The door opened again, this time all the way. Lynn was wearing baggy sweat clothes, as she always did in bed. They were gray and hung loose on her. Bright pink bunny slippers on her feet offset their drab color. Lynn's straight black hair hung down her back, the back she turned on me as soon as the door closed. I reset the chain and followed her into her living room, carrying my possessions.

"I'm sorry. It's a long story."

Lynn put her hands over her ears as she continued walking away from me and headed down a hallway. "I don't want to hear it now. I don't want to hear any of it. It's four in the morning, and I just want to go back to bed."

I took the hint and stopped apologizing. Instead, I looked for a place to park my suitcase and garment bag. I dumped them in a corner of the small living room. A moment later Lynn came padding back into the room carrying a couple of folded sheets, a blanket and a pillow. She handed them to me without a word and turned to the sofa. She bent down and tugged on a strap, and it unfolded into a modest-sized bed. That done, she headed to her own room.

"Thanks!" I called to her retreating back. Her hands went to her ears again in response.

I made up the futon, got undressed and tried to sleep, wondering how many days Lynn would be willing to put up with me. It didn't help that an hour later, sound asleep, I rolled too close to the edge of the futon frame, and the whole thing tipped over and dumped me onto the hardwood floor, then clattered back with a bang.

I was still untangling myself from the sheets when Lynn appeared.

"It tipped over," I said lamely.

She shook her head and went back to bed. I remade the bed and climbed back in. I guess I didn't put the futon on all the way because a second later it tipped over and dumped me to the floor again.

"Sorry!" I called out. Lynn didn't answer, and I managed to get through the rest of the night without it happening again.

Lynn let me sleep in when morning came. I was vaguely aware of her moving around, and at one point I heard her leave and then return about an hour later. Out for her morning run, I assumed, and went back to sleep. When I finally woke up it was nearly noon, and Lynn had left for her job as a stripper at The Pink Poodle. A note on the kitchen counter let me know there was one bagel left, some cream cheese in the refrigerator, and I was to rinse out the coffee pot after having what was left, please.

It's a strange feeling, being alone in a friend's apartment. So much of Lynn's personal life was unwittingly on display. It's a tiny apartment, just the front room with a little galley kitchen tacked onto one side, one bedroom, and a bathroom whose fixtures date back to a time when bellbottoms were first in style. The carpet was gone since the last time I was there, and now the original hardwood floors gave a warm hue to the room.

Lynn's apartment was on the second floor of a four-story building. From outside the open window over the kitchen sink came the sound of traffic from the street below along with the scent of garbage not yet collected. There was a short bookcase, and out of habit I scanned the titles. Lynn's reading tastes hadn't changed much. There were the usual historical romances, a few cocktail table books about foreign lands and a small stack of magazines about ballet. Judging from the dates on the magazines, Lynn must have let her subscription lapse over a year ago.

In the kitchen I found the half-dozen postcards I sent from Louisiana stuck to the refrigerator door with the last, the one letting her know of Eddie's death and my plans to return, on top.

After toasting and eating the bagel and finishing the coffee Lynn left for me, I washed and put away the few plates and cups that were in the sink and rinsed the coffee pot per direction. I took the sheets from the futon, folded them carefully, placed them with the pillow back in the closet, then folded up the bed again into a sofa. Only after all that did I shower, shave and get dressed, taking my suit from the garment bag and putting it on. My suit is an important tool in my profession, and I try to take care of it. I put on my watch and checked the time. It was almost one o'clock and time for me to get going.

I left Lynn's apartment, triple locked the flimsy door and dropped the keys in her mailbox. As I did, I wondered again just how welcome I was. I count Lynn as one of my few real friends and sometimes, just sometimes, wondered what life might have been like if we hadn't broken up.

A slight October breeze from the bay revived my spirits and scattered my melancholy as I emerged from Lynn's apartment building. I made a quick check to ensure there wasn't anyone waiting whom I wished to avoid, then crossed the street and headed for the bus stop. The sky was overcast with a touch of fog in the air, my favorite kind of weather and the best for my kind of work.

A bus came along within minutes, and I hopped on board, used my bus pass and found a place to stand and a strap to cling to. Like every city bus since their invention, it smelled of leather, diesel and sweat, and it groaned and swayed as the driver pulled away from the curb and back into traffic. There were seats available, but I like to ride standing up. It gives me a chance to look at people's faces and try to guess their stories. On a more practical note, it makes for a faster getaway if necessary.

I like taking the bus. I can learn all I need to know about a city and its mood, its beat, its rhythm and meter by riding public transportation. Besides, I don't own a car, let alone have a driver's license. I have no driver's license, no credit cards, at least not my own, no cell phone and most importantly, no police record. In general I try to live off the grid as much as possible. I figure the less known about me, the better.

It was so, so tempting to help myself to the wallets and other valuables that their owners unknowingly offered me on the bus as we headed downtown, but I managed to resist. I was after bigger game, and lifting wallets from out-of-town visitors is safer than from a local. Still, I looked longingly at all the coats hanging open and the other invitations.

A young woman with short, red-brown hair and a round, pretty face stood next to me, both of us clinging to straps and swaying in unison with the movement of the bus as we came near my stop. Her fashionable purse was unlatched, and I could see her wallet near the top. It would have been easy to pretend to lose my footing for a moment, bump into her and, misdirecting her attention by keeping eye contact with her all the while, let my hand dip in and out of her purse. It would have been so easy.

"Excuse me," She looked up. I leaned close to her so others nearby wouldn't hear. "Your purse is open." She looked down, quickly snapped it shut, and gave me a grateful smile.

"Gee, thanks." She had a nice smile. The bus lurched to a stop. I returned the smile.

"Don't mention it." I got off the bus having done my first and probably only good deed for the day.

I walked the last couple of blocks along Market Street to the Edgars Convention Center. It's a massive complex covering a full city block and surrounded by high-class hotels, restaurants, bars and cafes. Building that convention center required the destruction of a dozen or more ancient brick buildings and the businesses they housed. Its futuristic architecture of glass, concrete and steel had won numerous awards, and civic boosters hailed its construction as progress on the march. I see it as just another cookie cutter step toward making our city look like every other city in the country. But there's a silver lining to it, at least for me. When the economy is good, hardly a month goes by when there isn't a large industry conference or trade show held there, and that means opportunity for me.

I stopped walking and stood for a moment across Market from the main entrance and watched the activity across the street. A long line of taxis dropped off passengers. A steady stream of men and women in suits walked up the broad, white concrete steps and through the dozen or more glass doors. It reminded me of watching a nature film in grade school, one about worker bees and their hive. So much activity, so much rushing about, so many opportunities for me.

I turned and checked my reflection in the plate glass window of a travel agency. I certainly look the part of an honest conference attendee. I stand just a shade under six feet, and while I'm a bit thin, I have that healthy look that causes people to trust you. A haircut before my trip home made my sandy blond hair shorter than I prefer, but the conservative look and my clean-shaven face make it easier to blend in. As always, my suit, with its secret pockets hidden by expert tailoring, looked great.

I checked the time on my wristwatch. It was a nice souvenir from an electronics trade show a few years back. Its original owner must have paid some big bucks for it. It isn't really my style, a bit flashy, but it feels good on my wrist and does a good job of complementing my suit and supporting the image I try to convey. Unfortunately, I was going to have to hock the watch that evening if I wasn't successful today. That's just how desperate I was for money.

With my final checkout completed, I took a breath, dodged taxis and other traffic, crossed Market Street and joined the crowd at the conference center entrance. It was time for me to go to work.

CPSIA information can be obtained at www.ICGtesting.com
Printed in the USA
BVOW05s0530270514

354403BV00001B/3/P